one moment, one kiss…

The car was hot, and I felt even warmer against him. At one point, the train lurched, and we were shoved together even closer, my chest pressed against his.

I shut my eyes for a minute, not sure whether I wanted him to kiss me so we could get that first kiss over, or whether I was terrified because I had never wanted someone to kiss me so much in my entire life. And terrified that I didn't have a whole lot of kissing experience. I kept my eyes closed until we came to our stop. Then I opened them. He was staring at me. "Come on," he whispered.

Holding my hand, we slid through the crowd and up the steps to the street above.

✧ Other Books You May Enjoy ✧

illuminated

ERICA ORLOFF

speak

An Imprint of Penguin Group (USA) Inc.

SPEAK
Published by the Penguin Group
Penguin Group (USA) Inc., 345 Hudson Street, New York, New York 10014, U.S.A.
Penguin Group (Canada), 90 Eglinton Avenue East, Suite 700,
Toronto, Ontario, Canada M4P 2Y3 (a division of Pearson Penguin Canada Inc.)
Penguin Books Ltd, 80 Strand, London WC2R 0RL, England
Penguin Ireland, 25 St Stephen's Green, Dublin 2, Ireland
(a division of Penguin Books Ltd)
Penguin Group (Australia), 250 Camberwell Road, Camberwell, Victoria 3124, Australia
(a division of Pearson Australia Group Pty Ltd)
Penguin Books India Pvt Ltd, 11 Community Centre,
Panchsheel Park, New Delhi - 110 017, India
Penguin Group (NZ), 67 Apollo Drive, Rosedale, Auckland 0632, New Zealand
(a division of Pearson New Zealand Ltd.)
Penguin Books (South Africa) (Pty) Ltd, 24 Sturdee Avenue,
Rosebank, Johannesburg 2196, South Africa

Registered Offices: Penguin Books Ltd, 80 Strand, London WC2R 0RL, England

First published in the United States of America by Speak,
an imprint of Penguin Group (USA) Inc., 2011

1 3 5 7 9 10 8 6 4 2

Copyright © Erica Orloff, 2011
All rights reserved

LIBRARY OF CONGRESS CATALOGING-IN-PUBLICATION DATA IS AVAILABLE

Speak ISBN 978-0-14-241376-0

Printed in the United States of America

To my children, may each of you find something that means as much to you as the Book

illuminated

1

I had another dream . . . —A.

L ike the breath of a ghost against an icy window, the scrawl whispered to us across the centuries.

"Even a book has its secrets. Come on, then, tell us more," Uncle Harry spoke to the manuscript, as if willing it to illuminate. He leaned over its fragile pages like an ancient scholar, staring intently at the parchment.

"Secrets?" I asked him, my voice echoing in the cavernous room of the auction house, its marble floors and twenty-foot-high ceilings carrying even a soft hush like a tree rustling its leaves.

"Callie, everyone, everything, has secrets. Even books. My job is to coax them out." He aimed the ultraviolet light more closely and exhaled audibly.

"What is it?" I whispered, and peered over his shoulder, feeling a tingle like the delicate legs of a spider skittering up my neck and across my shoulders.

He pointed. "In the margin!"

And there, in a spidery scrawl, ethereal words emerged under the bluish light.

"It looks like someone wrote over old hand-writing," I said softly, squinting to make out the words. I knew that as the medieval illuminated manuscripts expert at Manhattan's Royal Auction House, Uncle Harry lived for these parchment books, illustrated by monks, that whispered stories from across the centuries. He talked about them over breakfast and over dinner. He read about them. He wrote about them. Whatever that writing was in the margin, it was the stuff of Uncle Harry's dreams.

"Do you know what this means?"

"Not really."

"It's a palimpsest."

"A what?"

He grinned at me. About six feet tall, with pale blue eyes and dimples, and just the first hints of silver strands in his sandy blond hair, Uncle Harry is the smartest man I know. He has a photographic memory and an encyclopedic knowledge of history. But he's not boring. With him, history is alive.

"A palimpsest! Centuries ago, a *thousand* years ago, paper was rare. So people wrote on papyrus or on goat skin or on vellum. They wrote on parchment and scrolls. Then, when they didn't need that book or information anymore, they washed out the old writing with oat bran and milk or some kind of wash, or sometimes a pumice stone. Then they would write on the parchment or vellum again. And the old writing was lost. They thought forever."

I stared at the feathery script in the margin barely visible in the glow of the bluish ultraviolet light.

"So I'm looking at hidden writing from a thousand years ago? That someone covered over. Secret writing?"

He nodded. "Sometimes we get lucky. The stars align, princess, and you get a gift...one of these. They're priceless. Usually time and the elements disintegrate them."

I stared at the book. The strokes in ink were precise, elegant, and each one perfect. No letter was higher than the other—they aligned, no ink blotches, each a work of art. The picture on the page was gilded, the gold not faded by time, and deep blues and greens depicted a knight and a lady, the colors as rich as a peacock's feathers.

"It is beautiful," I said.

"But what makes this even more extraordinary is the hidden writing. Secrets don't stay shrouded forever, Callie. Not really. They always leave a trail, even a thousand years later."

"Did the collector who brought it to the auction house know it was a palimpsest?"

He shook his head. "No. He inherited his father's collection of rare books and manuscripts. The son just wants the cash." Uncle Harry stared wistfully at the manuscript. "Little did he even imagine what secrets were on these pages. The auction for this will go into the hundreds of thousands of dollars, maybe millions. I'll have a better idea once I know more about the manuscript's history." He paused and shook his head. "It's rather sad, really."

"Why?"

"A person spends their whole life amassing a collection of books or antiques. They think it will help them live on forever. And then it gets sold by their kids, who don't really care one way or the other about their parents' stuff. Maybe an obsession can never be shared."

"Maybe. But then . . . here we are," I said. "The words in the margin have lived on. *You* care."

"I still can't believe it. And I know someone else who's going to be elated. I need to go call Dr. Peter Sokolov."

"Who's that?"

"He's a rare-book dealer. The world's foremost expert on medieval manuscripts."

"More of an expert than you? That's hard to believe."

"He was my mentor. And yes, he knows more than even I do. He's someone who understands your crazy old uncle and his love of these ancient papers." Uncle Harry kissed the top of my head. "I told you this was going to be a good summer."

I rolled my eyes. "All right. You found an old manuscript. A *really* old one. One that has secrets. But still I don't think you can count this as a good summer—yet. My father ditched me and took off for Europe with his latest blond girlfriend. Is it me or do they seem to be getting younger and blonder?"

"It's not you. I've never understood your father. Never understood why my sister married him in the first place." Uncle Harry frowned. "I shouldn't have said that."

"Why not? It's true. And as *exciting* as this is, it's, well, a dusty old manuscript." Could I tell him I was hoping for a summer romance? Or an adventure?

"Patience, Callie." He winked at me. "Secrets..."

"What's that supposed to mean?"

"You never know where a secret will take you. It's like playing hide-and-seek throughout history." He said it in a mysterious, yet playfully obnoxious kind of way. "I've got to go make some calls. You can look at the palimpsest. But don't touch it." He walked to his office, and with a backward glance added, "Or breathe on it."

I leaned over and stared at the tiny scrawl that was just barely visible. I squinted. The script was old-fashioned. I couldn't really make out any words.

Then I saw it. At the bottom it was signed.

···✦········✶···✳·············✶·········◇···☆···········◆····✶······

I had another dream, and this time the sun and moon and eleven stars were bowing down to me.

—A.

2

Touch the stars. Dream of them. —A.

My mother was my palimpsest. She died when I was six, and I've spent my life searching for hidden secrets about her, hoping she would whisper to me the way the scrawl in the margin whispered to Uncle Harry. It's a longing that never goes away. Sometimes, when I see one of my friends hug their mom, I feel an actual ache in my heart. That night, I curled my knees under me and pored over old photos of her when I was alone in my room in Harry's apartment.

My "room"—air quotes there—is what a Manhattan real estate agent calls a second bedroom—meaning it's not much more than an alcove where someone put up a wall. But it has space for me, and it's where I search for my mother's secrets. Uncle Harry has boxes of photos of my mom. He's my mother's brother, and I ask him questions about her all the time. I wonder if I am like her... because I know I'm nothing like my dad.

My father and I have spent our entire lives avoiding each other—in some ways, it's perfect for us that he's never home. During the school year, I lived with my father outside of Boston. Luckily, he travels so much I end up spending half my time with my friend Sofia's family, or being checked on by our neighbor in the condo across the hall. But summers are my favorite time, reserved for Uncle Harry and his partner, Gabe, and New York City. We usually fit in lots of plays, trips to the beach, and once, even a trip to Toronto.

And *this* summer? I was especially grateful to escape. This threatened to be the Summer of the Stepmother, since my dad had been checking out diamond rings with the latest, blondest girlfriend named Sharon. The whole concept kind of made me want to throw up.

After looking at photos of my mom and chatting on Facebook with Sofia, who was spending the summer at a show choir camp, I fell asleep with the TV turned low.

When I woke up, I stared at the ceiling, then looked at the plasma screen on the wall. A morning news anchor with hair perfectly plastered into place was telling me it was six A.M.

"Argh!" I said to Uncle Harry's cat, Aggie, short for Agamemnon. He has one green eye and one yellow, and is a silvery Persian who leaves hair everywhere. "It's summer. I can sleep in. *Why* am I awake?!"

Aggie just meowed and stepped on my stomach before settling down again, purring like a motor. I clicked channels with the remote, too lazy to get up, too awake to fall back to sleep.

About twenty minutes later, Uncle Harry knocked on my door. "You up?" he called.

"Unfortunately."

He poked his head in my room. "What are you wearing to work today?"

I looked over at my tiny closet, which was open and had my clothes spilling onto the floor. "Um . . . I don't know. Dressy jeans and a sweater set—it's so cold in your office, I'm tempted to wear mittens. And since when do you care what I wear to fetch your coffee? I'm your gopher. I haven't decided. It's too *early* to decide."

"What about this?" He flung a bag from Barney's at me.

I sat up and ruffled a hand through my bedhead mess of curls. I could hear Gabe singing in the shower—"Luck Be a Lady Tonight." He was once in a revival of *Guys and Dolls*. He had played Sky

Masterson. Uncle Harry went to the show twenty times, always sitting in the front row, center seat—which, if you do the math means he spent a small fortune—and he waited afterward with his yellow and black *Playbill* to get Gabe's autograph at the theater door. It's a nauseatingly cute "how we met" story. And the rest, as they say, is history.

It's pretty pathetic when your uncle has a better love story than you've had at this point. Being an affirmed member of the brainy club meant my love life definitely lacked something as adorable. Of course, my grandmother still thinks Uncle Harry just hasn't met the right woman. But at least he knows how to shop.

I peered into the bag, pushed aside the tissue paper, and looked up at Harry. "You're kidding, right?"

I pulled it out and held up the little black summer dress. It was, indeed, adorable. I glanced at the tag.

"*Three hundred and fifty dollars*? Now you've really lost your mind."

"No, I haven't. I've just always wanted to buy an Audrey Hepburn *Breakfast at Tiffany's* dress, but never had anyone to buy one for. Until you! Come on—don't you just *love* it?"

I nodded, shocked. It was probably the classiest thing I had ever owned. "It's gorgeous. Too bad you and a bunch of dusty manuscripts are the only ones to see me in it."

"You can never look too good for a day with goat skin and vellum."

I grinned at him. "Thank you. I really do love it."

After a shower, I let my hair air-dry curly. The weather report said humid—which means there is absolutely no point fighting my hair's true nature. Something that's a cross between a Chia pet and steel wool.

I put on some lip gloss and mascara and a pair of black ballet flats—I also don't fight being five feet three inches. But I'm cheating because really, it's five feet two, and my hair just adds a little height. My skin is naturally pale, with freckles that I also don't bother to fight very much, and I have light gray eyes. I looked over at the built-in bookshelves. Uncle Harry keeps a black-and-white framed photo of my mother. She's looking right at the camera and laughing, her hair blowing in the wind. In the picture, she's wearing this whole Madonna-in-the-'80s outfit, and somehow, she's pulling it off.

I wish I knew what was making her laugh in that picture. Uncle Harry doesn't remember. I look a little like her—different color hair, but the same pale skin. Alas, tanning just leaves me lobster-pinkish.

But I think that's where the similarity ends. Because somehow in every picture of her, she looks like a model, or a bohemian artist, or someone glamorous from a fairy-tale life.

I rechecked my reflection in the full-length mirror on the closet door in my room. I almost looked . . . adult. I smiled back at myself and then stepped out into the narrow hallway. It's lined with posters and Playbills from their favorite Broadway shows—*Guys and Dolls, Contact, 42nd Street, Chicago, Spamalot.* I turned right and walked into their kitchen to make some coffee. It's a big kitchen by Manhattan standards, tiny by Boston standards, with sparkling stainless appliances and gleaming pale maple cabinets and granite countertops. I started toward the coffeemaker.

"No time, sugarplum," Harry said. "Starbucks on the way. We've got to go."

Gabe walked over to me.

"Are you wearing a kimono?" I asked him, fingering the blue and green silk.

"Yup."

"Nice. I'll have to borrow it sometime."

"If I were you, I'd never change out of that to-die-for dress. You look gorgeous."

"Thanks." I stood on tiptoe and kissed him good-bye. "I liked the shower-chorus today."

"You could hear me?"

"Every note."

Harry playfully rolled his eyes. "He's a show-off. He knows darn well we can hear him."

After an elevator ride down forty stories to the lobby and a stop on the corner, Starbucks in hand (I would perish without my coffee—it's life juice), Harry and I walked through jostling morning crowds—but not toward the auction house.

"Where are we going?"

"To Dr. Sokolov's apartment."

"I thought he would come to the auction house so he could see it. Isn't this the kind of find you medieval scholars live for?"

Harry leaned his head back and laughed. "Impossible, I'm afraid."

"Why?"

"He's got agoraphobia."

I tried to remember which phobia that was.

Harry glanced over, "He never leaves his brownstone. *Ever.*"

"Ever? Does he work?"

"He does research and writes. He lectures a

satellite class—beamed into the classroom at NYU. He also does podcasts. Technology is a friend to people like him. And people bring books to him. Or in my case, I'll be sending video."

"That's weird. Not leaving the house. How does he get food?"

"Callie, honey. This is New York. Everything is delivered."

I thought of the thirty deli, Chinese, Italian, Indian, and even Ethiopian menus in the junk drawer in the kitchen. "All right, then, there must be *some* things he has to leave the house for."

"Maybe. But he has an assistant."

We hailed a yellow cab and about ten white-knuckle-defying, near-pedestrian-hitting minutes later stood outside a four-story brownstone down in Greenwich Village. On either side of the street, trees stretched toward sky, their leaves arching over the road, trying to escape their concrete confines. Two long, sleek black limousines double-parked outside other brownstones.

"This street is beautiful," I said, climbing out of the cab. "It's a part of New York that feels secret." I looked up at Harry.

"That building is where a certain A-list actress

lives. I can't tell you how many times I've been here and spotted Uma Thurman. Oh, and my big crush, Anderson Cooper. Saw him on his bike here once." He nodded toward a three-story brick building across the street. "I think some famous writer lives there. Anyway, Dr. Sokolov is, as they say, old money. His family has owned this brownstone for a hundred years or more. Since back when horses and buggies drove through here. Oh, want a fun, gross fact from history?"

"I'm not sure."

"It has to do with the brownstones. The reason they're multiple stories is so way back when, the rich could live on the top floors away from the stench of horse manure. It was—"

"Stop right there," I groaned. Sometimes, Harry's love of history is just a little too graphic for me.

I looked up and down the street and wondered what it would be like to live there. The street was serene, and I felt transported to another time. I could even hear birds chirping in the trees. I faced Dr. Sokolov's door. A small sign by the bell said SOKOLOV & SONS, ANTIQUARIANS. Harry pressed the doorbell, and it chimed deeply.

The door—fourteen feet high, polished to a sheen,

and probably inches thick—swung back, but instead of some agoraphobic old book expert, I found myself face-to-face with the most gorgeous guy I'd ever seen in my life. I think I turned ten shades of scarlet.

"Hey, Harry." He smiled at my uncle, revealing two deep chasmlike dimples in his cheeks. Then he stared at me. And I thought I felt him stare through me. Or inside me. I took a small step backward and bumped into Uncle Harry.

"Calliope, this is August Sokolov. The esteemed Dr. Sokolov's assistant—and his son."

"Hi," I managed to breathe.

There was a long silence. In that time, I noticed his eyes were green and his brown hair curled a bit at the collar of his shirt. And he had an earring—a yin-and-yang symbol. And a scar in a little horseshoe shape near his left eye. He stared at me. Then he blinked and said, "Come on in. My dad's waiting."

I stepped inside, Uncle Harry behind me. As August led us through a marble-floored foyer, I glared over my shoulder at my uncle as we walked past paintings and even an honest-to-God suit of armor.

What? Uncle Harry mouthed silently, too innocent for words, batting his eyes.

But I kept glaring.

Audrey Hepburn dress, indeed. He was just a little too obvious. He could have warned me, at least.

August ushered us into a huge study with ceilings eighteen feet high. The walls were lined with bookshelves, which in turn were filled with book after book—most of them leather-bound and ancient-looking. A tall ladder with a hook on the top and wheels at its base used to reach the uppermost shelves leaned against the far wall.

A man in a rumpled white shirt sat behind an immense desk surrounded by papers and file folders, silver-rimmed glasses perched on the end of his nose. He stood the minute we walked in, revealing equally wrinkled, coffee-stained khakis. He resembled August, right down to his longish hair and high cheekbones, only older. And messier.

"Harry." He beamed. "Is it true?"

Uncle Harry nodded. "I saw the words myself. So did Callie. My niece. Callie, this is Professor Sokolov."

"Call me Peter."

I said hello and stood by trying not to look at August as Uncle Harry launched into the story of the palimpsest—and soon they were poring over old books. I didn't want to look bored. But really, after twenty-four hours of palimpsest talk, I felt like I could have told the whole story of the manuscript by heart.

August came and leaned close to me. "In about one minute," he whispered, his breath hot on my neck, "they will be so involved talking about their work that they won't notice we've left. Come on, let's go to the garden. I promise to be more interesting."

I glanced at Uncle Harry. He was describing the palimpsest in detail to Professor Sokolov. A bomb could have exploded next to him and he wouldn't have noticed.

I nodded and followed August through the house and out a set of French doors to a garden filled with roses in shades of red, pink, yellow, and a pale purple. In one corner, a small pagoda-style greenhouse stood, its glass fogged from the humidity inside. In another corner an enormous aviary rose skyward.

"Wow," I exhaled.

"Better than medieval manuscript talk, right?"

I nodded. "The manuscript is amazing, though, even if I don't know much about it," I said. "I saw the hidden words."

"My father didn't sleep last night, he was so excited."

"I'm not sure if Harry did, either."

"What about you?" He looked at me playfully.

Was he flirting with me? Guys never did this with brainy girls. I was on track to be valedictorian. My average was a 4.3. I was going to kill Uncle Harry. I tried to think of a snappy comeback, but settled on the very lame, "I slept fine. Well, except for waking up at six when I could have slept in."

"I'm a vampire myself."

"Really?" I smiled at him. "Should I be worried?" *Okay, not a bad line.*

"No. I promise not to bite. But I will stay up all night and sleep all morning. Today was an exception—the palimpsest and all."

"So you know all about them?"

"Yeah. But you don't get to see one often. But I took you out here to escape boring book talk. All right, change of subject. Are you visiting, or do you live in New York?"

"Visiting. I spend every summer here. My dad and I live in Boston. What about you?"

"I was born here. In this house, actually. My mother did this weird bathtub birth."

"Really?" I raised one eyebrow. I was quite positive that if I ever had a baby when I got married, I was going to ask for all the drugs the doctors would give me.

"Yeah. Born in the upstairs bathtub. My mother had two friends chanting, a midwife named Heavenly and my poor dad, who just wanted me born in a regular hospital. So yeah, I took my first breath in this house. Lived here my whole life, just like Dad. I take classes at NYU, work for my dad. He hopes I go into the family business."

"Illuminated manuscripts?"

"Sort of. Manuscripts. First editions. Rare-book dealer."

"The sign said 'and sons.' Do you have brothers?"

He shook his head. "My father is actually the 'and sons.' He and his brother went into the family business—that had been my grandfather's. My uncle died ten years ago. So now it's just my dad. And me. 'And son.' But I really want to be a writer. Write *new* books, not collect old ones."

"But you're his assistant."

He nodded. "For now. I don't know. I love the old books. But not the way he does. My father has his manuscripts. *This* is my passion," August said. He folded his arms across his chest and smiled as he gazed across the gardens. "I write over there." He gestured to a wooden table with a MacBook on it.

"It's beautiful. Did you really plant all this, make this garden?"

"Sort of. My grandmother kept a garden, but it was neglected over the years. I guess I've just brought it back to life. I like being outside. Since my father won't leave the house, I had to sort of make my own vacation spot. Right here."

"Will he at least come out here?"

August shook his head.

I walked to the aviary, which was filled with birds as jewel-colored as the flowers. "They're gorgeous. What kind of birds are they?"

The birds didn't sing so much as titter. One landed on a branch near me, its feathers turquoise, emerald, and ruby-colored.

"They're Gouldian finches," August said. "From Australia."

"But what about those?" I pointed to plain brown ones. They weren't nearly as exotic.

In a quiet voice, he said, "Gouldians aren't usually very good parents. So the society finches step in and raise the hatchlings. They're like finch nannies."

"Sounds like me. I had a nanny until I started high school. And even then, I had to beg not to have one."

August looked at me. "Ah, we have more in common than a palimpsest. Me, too. My Gouldian mother flew the coop when I was ten. Divorced my dad."

"So where's your mother now?"

"California. She couldn't handle Dad's eccentricities. Or motherhood, for that matter. Bathtub birth aside, after that, she wanted to 'find herself.'" He did the air-quote thing.

"And your dad...does it bother you..." I trailed off. I didn't want to seem nosy. But *never* leaving the house?

He shook his head. "He's brilliant, you know. And that's just how he is. I guess I don't know him any other way. So I don't miss him being something else. What about your family?"

I nodded and pointed at a bird with an azure-crested chest. "My dad is the Gouldian then. My mom...she died when I was in kindergarten. So it's my uncle Harry who's like that one," I pointed to a bird preening a baby. "He's the one who takes care of me. Even when I'm in Boston, we talk almost every day. We Skype. He flies or takes the train up every couple of weeks. I come down on weekends when I can."

I watched the birds dart from nest to nest. "I like this better than manuscripts. My uncle—you should have *seen* him when the words showed up in the margins."

"If it really is a palimpsest...it's the find of a lifetime. You can't blame them."

I smiled at him. "No, I can't. I don't know if I have anything that I would feel that way over. Kind of like finding a treasure chest."

"It is. That's the part of Sokolov and Sons I like *a lot*. The mystery of it all. Who owned the books, where they came from. Stumbling on a rare first edition. It's kind of like there's a story in every book. The story inside the pages, and the story *of* the book. The books remind me of my father. To know him, you have to come into *his* world. To know a book, you have to enter it."

I heard a splash behind us and turned around.

"Someone's hungry." August laughed.

"What?"

"Come over here." August led me to a huge industrial barrel, cut in half, with water flowing into it like a waterfall.

"My koi pond. Manhattan style."

I watched gold-speckled fat fish swim lazily, occasionally flicking their tails and changing direction. I touched my fingers to the cool water.

"If I had a garden like this, I would never leave it. I can't believe your father won't come out and enjoy it."

"He looks at it from the doors sometimes. He's proud of me, of what I did out here."

A fish came up to the surface and seemed to kiss the air.

"That's Zen. He'll eat from your hand. He's the splasher. Here." August opened a plastic container and handed me a few pellets of fish food. I took one and held it down to the water, and Zen kissed my fingertips with a puckered movement and took it from me. I forgot, for a moment, that I was in Manhattan, the city I love that never sleeps and is always moving and making noise.

"I would sleep out here, if I could. It's so peaceful."

"Sometimes I do." August pointed at a hammock. "Want to take a nap?" he asked playfully.

I flushed. "Um, I just had Starbucks. Not sleepy." I bit my lip. *Smooth one, Callie.* Fumbling for a recovery, I said, "You look like your dad a lot."

"Yeah. I know."

"So . . . how did your dad get that way?" As soon as I asked, I felt bad. Maybe he didn't like talking about it. "I'm sorry. I just meant afraid of leaving the house."

"No, it's okay. It's nice you ask. I think, for him, he had a panic attack one day. In the middle of Washington Square Park. For no reason other than . . . he did. And then he had another when he and I were eating pizza at this place down the street. And then he had another. And another. And once in a classroom. In the middle of a lecture. And about the only place he *never* had a panic attack was home. With his books. And so he avoided the park and then the classroom, and then the bodega down the street . . . and little by little his world got smaller. Until now he's kind of like my birds. Trapped in his world, but happy, in a way. He loves his life."

"Doesn't he ever wish he could come out here and smell the flowers?"

August shook his head. "No. He's gotten used to how he is. He likes smelling old books. He likes Eau de Musty."

I laughed. "But this is so perfect. Harry's apartment has a balcony, and we have one measly fern that the three of us forget to water. Then I'll remember and practically drown the poor thing. That's about it. But this . . ."

"Well, anytime you want to visit and lie in the hammock . . . you're welcome to come. And I promise, not one word about old books."

"Thanks. Maybe I will."

"One more thing to show you." He led me to the little greenhouse. He opened the door, and humid air enveloped me like a wet kiss. We ducked inside, my head bowing at the low doorway. Once inside, there was a quiet hum of a fan, and the door was shut, leaving the greenhouse so hot that droplets of humidity clung to me. We had to stand close, almost touching, because the pagoda was so small.

"These are my orchids," he whispered, facing me, my chest almost touching his. The air was fragrant, and I could smell the flowers, but could also smell August, his own scent that clung to him. For a long moment, we stared at each other. I thought he might kiss me, and the thought made me panic. I looked away first.

"Come on," he said. "Let's go see what Harry and my dad are up to."

We left the greenhouse, the outside summer air feeling cool after the pagoda. I followed August into the house, reluctantly leaving the bird sounds and the koi. Reluctantly leaving a place where I was alone with him.

3

Is love so different from a shooting star,
passing violently through the night sky?
—A.

"August?" Professor Sokolov looked up when we returned. "Where did you disappear to?"

"Garden."

"I needn't have asked." He looked at me. "What better way to impress our beautiful guest. But August, Callie, this is the discovery of a *lifetime*. We have work to do."

"We?" I looked at Uncle Harry. My skin still felt damp from the greenhouse, and my heart still pounded from being so close to August. I wondered if Uncle Harry could hear it beating. If August knew how he affected me.

"Professor Sokolov is going to help me research the origins of the palimpsest. Which means August here will be doing the actual research. And I'm sending *you* to represent the Royal Auction House and me. You *are* a summer intern after all."

"But why me? Why not you?" I asked. I was a gopher. I got coffee. I made sure Uncle Harry's Starbucks was made perfectly—caramel macchiatto with soy milk, light on foam, two raw sugar packets. I made copies. I sent e-mails. I typed reports. I had a job at an impressive place to make my college applications look really good—the Royal Auction House was legendary. But I wasn't a researcher. Though the prospect of treasure hunting with August meant my summer just got a whole lot more interesting.

"My job is to continue to discover just what this mysterious A. has to say. Yours is to follow the trail. I trust you." He stared at me meaningfully. Like, *Why are you arguing when you get to be with August?*

"Uh, what sort of work are we going to be doing?"

"When a manuscript is centuries old, it has passed through many hands. Remember when I said it had secrets?"

I nodded.

"It has a story, too. And we need to know that story."

Dr. Sokolov pulled a book off of his shelf. "You see this volume? It is a book of poems by Walt Whitman. A first edition." He handed it to me. "Open the front cover. Carefully."

The cover was worn and tattered, a plain brown with gold foil letters proclaiming *Leaves of Grass*. The spine was stiff and the pages very brittle. "How old is it?"

"It was published in 1889," August said. He stood to my side as I opened the book.

On the front page was an inscription. At the bottom was a name in ink . . . Walt Whitman.

"He signed this?" I asked.

Dr. Sokolov smiled. "That little book is worth about thirteen thousand dollars. But the path we traveled to discover it and certify that it was truly signed by Whitman . . . well, that path was almost as worn as the book."

I felt a tingle rush through me. "It really is like a mystery, isn't it?" I shut the book and held it out. "Please take it before I accidentally rip a page." I flunked out of ballet class—gracefulness was *not* my thing, Audrey Hepburn little black dress aside.

August leaned close to me. "We trust you," he teased.

Uncle Harry said, "It's like unraveling a secret thread through time. You start with what you know: The book was brought in by a family wanting to sell the entire collection. They acquired the palimpsest from someone, somewhere. We need to find out who and where. You start unraveling through history."

I looked over at my uncle. "I've never done anything like this." I'd helped at the auction house, and I'd helped him at home, doing a little fact-checking. I'd gone to the New York City public library, the big stone lions out front greeting me, and combed the reference section, but finding out where the palimpsest was from? I looked at August.

"Don't worry," he said. "It'll be fun." He leaned in close and whispered, "You and me. On the hunt for a secret author. I could think of worse ways to spend the summer."

Professor Sokolov smiled at his son. "What are you two whispering about?"

August shrugged.

"Another thing," Harry said. "The reason I'm sending you, Callie, is we want this kept quiet."

"Quiet? Why?"

"Because you don't announce something like this until you know what you have. You two can do some snooping without it seeming like official auction house business. We have to find out who A. was and when he lived."

"Who said it was a he?" I asked. "Maybe it's a she."

"She has a point, Harry," Professor Sokolov said.

"Yes, yes. Either way, it's completely quiet. We

don't tip our hand. If you think anyone is going to be pleased that they let, in essence, a priceless palimpsest slip through their fingers. It could be dangerous. People don't take kindly to fortunes lost and found."

"Fortunes lost and found. It sounds more and more like a treasure hunt," I said.

"Treasure hunt and detective story rolled into one," said August.

And maybe romance and intrigue, I thought to myself, sneaking a glance at him.

August said, "Come on. I'll give you my e-mail and cell phone number. I have a card in my office."

I followed him. His office was a small room down the hall. Inside, it reminded me of his garden— terrariums and pots of green plants sat on the windowsill; a goldfish swam lazily in a giant bowl. "When he gets bigger can he join the fish in the pond out back?"

"I don't know. I kind of like having Albert to talk to."

"Albert?" I raised one eyebrow.

He shrugged. "Einstein. What can I say? The fish and I discuss relativity . . . and beautiful girls."

I felt my cheeks redden.

He handed me a business card. "That's my e-mail and my cell phone number."

"Do you have your cell?"

He handed me his phone, and I punched in my e-mail address, IM screen name, and cell phone number and handed it back to him.

"Meet you tomorrow at the auction house. Nine o'clock?"

I nodded. "Sure."

"We should be prepared—you never know where a manuscript will lead you."

I was already thinking that. Then I heard Uncle Harry calling me.

"I better go," I said. I felt like my heart was loud enough to echo off the ceiling.

I found Uncle Harry in the hall and waved good-bye to August. When we were outside, Uncle Harry smirked.

"What?" I demanded.

"I knew that Audrey Hepburn dress would do the trick."

"You could have warned me. You could have *told me* that Dr. Sokolov had a gorgeous son. Drop-dead gorgeous." *Seriously drop-dead gorgeous.* He was cuter than any guy in my entire school.

"No, I couldn't. Because then you would have been all worried and freaked out. You would have avoided this, just like you didn't go to your junior prom, and you wouldn't agree to that blind date with the grandson of the lady in 2B. You, Callie, are a chicken when it comes to dating. This was a lot better."

"A lot better? So . . . this was a plan?"

We walked side by side up to the avenue to catch a cab.

"Well, it's not like I *knew* the book was a palimpsest, if that's what you're asking." He raised his hand to hail a yellow taxi. "But I would have figured out some excuse to get you down here. I don't know why I didn't think of setting the two of you up before."

"But now, there's really a reason—a mystery."

"You sound kind of excited. I thought goat skins and vellum and dusty manuscripts were boring."

"No, this is different. It's a hunt. It's . . . it's a mystery: Who is *A.?*"

"And you're not excited the slightest bit about sleuthing with August."

A cab pulled over to pick us up. I had August's card in my hand. I glanced over at Uncle Harry. "Well, if I have to sleuth this summer and play Nancy Drew . . . there's nothing like a hot guy to make it even more interesting."

As I slid into the cab, I smiled. The Summer of the Palimpsest was shaping up to be very interesting.

4

Does love start with a secret? —A.

The next morning at nine, I was drinking my second cup of coffee (what would I do without caffeine?) when August strode into the auction house. He wore a button-down and nice jeans, and he waved when he saw Uncle Harry and me. My stomach did a flip.

"So is that it?" He pointed at the manuscript, which was now safely encased under glass.

I nodded. He leaned over the case and peered down. "Have you looked at it more? What sort of person is this A.?"

"I don't know," Harry said. "Romantic. Seems fascinated by stars and the sun."

"I think I'm going to like A. I like the stars and sun myself," August said, glancing my way.

I flicked on the special UV light. "See. Look at the lettering."

When August exhaled, the glass fogged slightly. I could see, up close, his eyes change in the light as he peered into the case. The lettering was faint and pale bluish under the special light.

I pointed. "On that page, there's a quote about eleven stars and the sun and the moon bowing down."

He smiled at me slyly. "Well, then he's more than a fan of the stars—our A. is a biblical scholar."

"How do you know that?" I asked.

"That quote is from Genesis."

"Yes," Harry said. He leaned over to me and whispered in my ear, "Pity he's so dumb."

Shut up, I mouthed.

Harry stood upright again. "Well, kids, I contacted James Rose, the man whose collection we are auctioning off. You two are meeting him in his apartment at ten thirty." Harry handed me an address written on a piece of notepaper. "Remember, we don't want to let on too much. Not yet. Just try to get him to talk a little about the origins of the collection. You can say that we think one or two of the books might be extremely rare. Particularly this one. See where it leads you. His father may have acquired it not knowing what he had. Or he may have acquired it illegally. Antiquities are sometimes sold from private collection to private collection. Sometimes the origins are a bit nefarious."

"People steal rare books?" I asked.

Harry nodded vigorously. "There's even one sneaky thief they call the Tome Raider."

"You have *got* to be kidding me," I said, laughing.

"I'm not. It's a secretive world—who reads and collects books like these? Museums, auction houses, libraries . . . and collectors. And the people who collect them are often obsessive and possessive. I know of one woman—I won't name names, but she is on the society pages every week in this city. And she is absolutely obsessed with *Little Women*. She will pay any price for first editions—she owns seven of them already that I know of. I think people who develop these collections are often hunting for feelings. For solace."

"What do you mean?" I asked.

"People who love books, who collect these kinds of books, they're often seeking to re-create the feelings the books inspired in them. That society woman? My guess is *Little Women* was some sort of comfort to her in a lonely boarding-school existence, and now she has the money to acquire them. And some will stop at nothing. The histories of these books and how they came to be in the hands of who has them isn't always a straight line. And sometimes it's not even a legal one."

"I feel like a spy or something. So does this address self-destruct in ten seconds?" I asked, holding up the paper.

"No. But *you* may if you don't get going. Oh, and I know August has a near-photographic memory, so just try to remember everything this guy says. Don't take notes."

"Why?"

"People hold back when you take notes. They suddenly worry that if they say something it's going to come back and haunt them."

"Okay. Come on, August."

He was still bent over the manuscript.

"August?"

"Sorry. But A. seems like a lonely guy . . . I feel like I know him."

"Again"—I crossed my arms—"couldn't A. be a girl?"

August looked back at the manuscript. "I don't think so. The handwriting . . . I think it's male."

I rolled my eyes. "Please. How can you know if handwriting is male or female?"

August grinned at me, showing his dimples. "All

right, then. A. is simply A. Not male. Not female. Not until we know for sure."

"Thank you." I smiled back at him.

"Well," Uncle Harry said, "it would be good if we could find out for sure who A. is. If we could actually tie the palimpsest to a person in history, it would make this find even more incredible, and even more valuable. Now off you go."

The two of us left the auction house. "The address is only thirty blocks away," I said to August. "Want to walk it?" He nodded, and we set off on foot.

"How come you didn't come back to the garden last night?" he asked.

"Was I supposed to?" I asked, raising an eyebrow.

"I thought my hint about the hammock would be enough to lure you back." He smiled at me. "I slept out there last night. Kind of hoping you'd show up."

"But . . ." I'd never met a guy this forward before, and I kind of liked it.

"Not enough of a specific invitation?"

"Maybe." I playfully pouted by sticking out my bottom lip slightly.

"Don't do that . . . I'd have to give you the moon, the world, anything you wanted with a look like that."

My nerves were getting the best of me. Part of

me wanted to keep looking at him, and part of me wanted to run away. When he grinned, he looked like a little boy. When he was serious, he looked very much like a young college professor, studious and thoughtful. Either way . . . he was gorgeous.

We fell into step with each other.

"So, Calliope. You're going into your senior year?" he asked me.

"Yes."

"Where do you want to go to college?"

"That's a loaded question."

"Why?"

I shrugged. "My father wants me to go to Harvard. He would like me to be pre-law. Follow in his footsteps. Inherit the firm. Beat people up in a courtroom for a living."

"And you?"

"I'd like to study English literature or philosophy, or history, like my uncle. None of which, of course, I can do anything useful with, according to my father. I'd like to study *anything* but law."

"Have you told him?"

"You don't tell my dad anything. No one tells him anything. Or you do, but he barrels on as if he didn't hear you. Most of the time, I feel like I am filing a motion with the judge when I talk to him." I *really* wanted to change the subject. Somehow August seemed to pick up on my mood.

"My father would like me to study medieval history. But he seems to understand I'd rather be out back in my garden writing. Funny" —he dug his hands into his pocket—"at NYU, you meet kids with all kinds of families, and sometimes, I'm struck by the fact that I should be jealous of some of them. 'Normal' families. You know, the kind that can actually leave the house together. Mom, dad, two-point-four children, dog. But I'm not. My dad lets me be whoever I want." He laughed.

"What?"

"Well, even when I was in high school . . . what was he going to do if I didn't listen to him? He could ground me. But if I left the house anyway, it wasn't like he would come running after me."

"So did you do that?"

He shook his head. "Not my style. Dad and I get each other."

We walked past huge window displays of fashion, a few galleries, bakeries, delis. Eventually, we arrived at the gleaming building where James Rose lived.

"Here we go. Ascending to the lion's den," August whispered.

The thought was unsettling, yet also attractive. Kind of like August. "Why do you say that?"

"This isn't my first manuscript hunt. Think Indiana Jones with less scruples. Private sales often hide the provenance."

"You mean where they got it from?"

He nodded. "Especially if it should be in a museum and not a private collection."

A doorman in a dark blue uniform with gold braiding on the pockets, shoulders, and lapel, opened the shining brass and glass door. A concierge at a marble desk took our names and lifted a phone and said, "Please inform Mr. Rose that he has two visitors, a Mr. Sokolov and a Ms. Martin. Yes."

He replaced the phone on its receiver. "Penthouse," he told us, and pointed to the elevators.

"We'll take the stairs," August said.

I stared at him.

The concierge looked at him strangely. "It's forty-five floors, sir."

"That's okay."

I think my mouth actually dropped.

The doorman pointed to a far door in the lobby that had a brass plaque that read STAIRWELL. I followed August as he nonchalantly headed for the door. He was halfway up the first flight when I, already *slightly* out of breath, asked, "Is there some reason why we have to walk forty-five flights?"

"I've got this thing about elevators."

He said it matter-of-factly, but I followed him wondering if he was slightly crazy, or at least had inherited a tiny bit of his dad's illness. I didn't love elevators. I sometimes wondered, when one jolted a little as it arrived at my floor, if it might snap a cable and plummet, sending me to a spectacular death below (okay, so I can be dramatic). I sometimes worried about electric grid blackouts, like the one that had happened the previous summer, trapping people in elevators and on subway cars.

But given a choice between forty-five flights of stairs and a possible snapped cable, I was taking the elevator.

By flight twenty-five, I had to stop and catch my breath. "I . . ." I panted, "won't be . . . abl. . . . to spea. . . . when we get there."

"I'll do the talking in the beginning."

He was shockingly not winded. And he saw my look and shrugged. "I do this all the time." Finally, sweating and sucking air, legs slightly rubbery, I arrived, with August, at the forty-fifth floor. If he wasn't so cute, I would have killed him.

He patiently waited while I caught my breath,

and then we walked down a marble-tiled hushed hallway with only two apartments on it, to James Rose's 45A. August knocked, and it was opened by a butler—or at least what I assumed was one—in a pressed uniform. He was an older gentleman, and as he led us into the living room, I leaned over and whispered to August, "It's like Batman's Alfred."

We were shown into a room that was bigger than a bowling alley and overlooked Central Park from every window—all of which rose from nearly the floor to the ceiling and shone in the summer sun.

The apartment was stark. Modern sculptures of bronze and other metals emerged out of the floor like alien creatures clawing out of someone's stomach. There were few pieces of furniture—one sleek couch in all white and a matching chair. The place was cooled to a temperature more appropriate for a polar bear—which I actually appreciated, considering my calf-aching, thigh-busting hike to get there.

James Rose emerged from another room. I guess I was expecting a man who befitted an apartment like that. I was expecting Bruce Wayne.

Instead, we got the Penguin. A short, squat man with birdlike features.

"Hello," he said. I thought he was talking to us, but then I noticed the Bluetooth headset in his ear.

Apparently, we weren't going to get his undivided attention. He barely glanced at us as he paced.

"Mr. Rose," August began, "we're appraising the collection, which is most impressive. And we were wondering if your father left any information on the illuminated manuscript. The one with the thick pages—the Book of Hours."

"Hold on," James Rose said into his earpiece. "I don't know anything about the book you're asking about. To be honest, I don't know anything about the entire collection. And neither did my father."

I shook my head slightly, "But he had—"

James Rose lifted a hand and cut me off. "No. The collection actually belonged to my mother. It was her passion. But when they got divorced, my father got it in the settlement. I don't know anything about the books. I collect twentieth-century sculpture. I manage the family trust. I just want the proceeds from the auction. I'm not interested in the book. I can't help you."

"Well, could we talk to your mother?" I asked.

"Sure. If you can find her. We don't speak. I don't know where she is."

I exchanged glances with August. He said, "Thanks for your time, Mr. Rose. If you think of anything that might help us, here's the card for the auction house. You can speak to this man." He handed him Uncle Harry's business card, on a thick ivory vellum stock with raised gold lettering.

"Whatever. Listen . . . I have to take this."

He turned, not even bothering to say good-bye.

"Well, that was a waste," I said to August. "Not to mention an agonizing forty-five-floor climb to have the guy tell us *nothing*."

"Well, not nothing." August moved closer to me. My heart started beating like I had just climbed the stairs. How could someone I'd just met yesterday have this kind of effect on me? "His mother is the one who loved the collection. If she's like every other collector I've ever met, she knows every scrap of history about the book. *Someone* cared about this collection."

"So where is she?"

Alfred the non-Batman butler returned to escort us to the door.

"I don't know," August said. "But she's somewhere, right? She didn't just vanish. We find her, we find a piece to our puzzle."

We followed Alfred out of the apartment and started the long walk down the stairs. My calves burned.

"August?"

"Hmm?"

"You don't *ever* ride in elevators?"

"Nope."

I sighed. We kept descending, the stairwell hot and stuffy and smelling of concrete. We finally arrived at the door to the lobby. When we pushed it open, Rose's butler was standing there with a bag of trash.

"Here," he whispered, and thrust a piece of paper in my hand. "He thinks I'm taking the garbage to the incinerator."

I looked down at the piece of paper.

MIRIAM ROSE
448 Shore Hollow Lane
Ocean Beach, NY

"Thank you," I said gratefully.

"Mrs. Rose was the most decent woman I've ever known. I was with her for twenty years. Her husband was horrid . . . their son not much better. And it would crush her if the manuscript was sold. It meant everything to her. Let her know it's being auctioned."

"We will," August said.

"Thank you. I better return before he gets suspicious."

"One more thing," August said.

"Yes?"

"Does he really have no idea where she is?"

"Of course he knows where she is. He doesn't want you alerting her about the collection."

"Thanks."

As August and I walked across the lobby, I asked him, "Why did you want to know that?"

"Because that means Rose at least knows the collection is worth something. Something more than a bunch of pages. To someone. Means, I'm sure, that he knew it was more than a simple Book of Hours before we ever got there. That book belongs in a museum, not locked away where no one cares about it."

"Poor A.," I murmured.

"Why do you say that?"

"A.'s secrets. Hidden away. I think A. had something to say. It's like he wanted us to know something. Wanted the world to know. Whatever it is, we should find out. Someone should know about A."

"You said 'he.'"

I laughed. "Or *she*." But as I thought about it, somehow I *knew* A. was a guy. The doorman opened the door for us, and we walked out into the noonday sun.

"We don't need to be back anytime soon. Want

to take a detour to Central Park for lunch?" August asked.

"Sure," I said.

We walked toward the park, the sun strong and steady. As we stepped through the entrance near the Museum of Natural History, the trees shaded us.

"Hot dog?" August asked, pointing to a vendor beneath a blue striped umbrella.

"I'm so going to regret this, but yeah."

August ordered us two hot dogs and two Cokes. "Let's go to Turtle Pond," he said.

"I don't know that I've ever been to it."

"Come on." We took our food and walked side by side. "The best thing about Turtle Pond is that it's designated as a quiet area. No loud music. No skaters. Just turtles."

We arrived at the pond, and except for the skyscrapers in the distance, you could forget you were in the middle of Manhattan. We found a flat rock and sat down. I slipped off my sandals and stretched my legs.

August kicked off his sneakers. He ate his hot dog and sipped his soda. As we were sitting, a green turtle poked its head out of the water near the shoreline and began pulling itself up on a log.

"You should get a turtle for your garden," I said.

"I actually thought of that." He laughed. "But a box turtle can live sixty or seventy years. We're talking a big commitment here. It would be like Sokolov and Sons and Turtle."

A yellow butterfly flitted near my feet, then rose up and toward my face before fluttering away.

August stared at me, and for a moment our eyes caught. He was so sexy, and still, there was something in the way he looked at me, something behind his gaze that made me flush. I prayed the sun had already reddened my face so he wouldn't see.

He rolled onto his back and stared up at the sky at the clouds. "I see a camel."

I looked up. Which was better than looking at him and feeling flustered. "I see it. All right, over there. A cherub. See it?"

"Yeah. But look at that." He pointed.

"What do you think it looks like?"

"You tell me."

I leaned back on my hands and studied the cloud. "I don't know."

"It's a palimpsest."

I playfully slapped his arm. "Sure."

"Come on! A. is trying to tell us something."

"Oh, yeah . . . okay, August."

"A. is saying 'Come find me.'"

I leaned forward and wrapped my arms around my legs, resting my chin on my knees. "I see it now," I played along. "Look. The cloud's shape is changing. It looks like a question mark now. A. is saying, 'Figure out the mystery.'"

"Now you're talking, Callie. And you know, you can't go back to Boston until we figure it out."

"We have eight weeks." *Eight weeks,* I told myself. Then I would go back to my real life in Boston. If this turned into anything . . . it was a summer thing. I heard my father's mantras for me. *Calliope, be reasonable. Calliope, be practical. Calliope, keep your eye on the prize.*

"What if we can't figure it out in eight weeks?"

"That's all I have." I needed to face reality. Eight weeks.

"Well, then we better get going." He stood up and held out a hand to pull me up from the rock. I took it and felt all wobbly inside again.

I slipped my sandals back on and looked up at the cloud. It transformed from our fantasy back to being a wisp of fluff and not really looking like anything.

5

I long. —A.

"Okay, you two will be heading out to pay a visit to Miriam Rose," Harry said, holding up the strip of paper we had gotten from the butler. "I called her. I know Miriam. I've met her at a few society functions, a charity ball one year. Of course, that was when she was still married. Before she became a New York society pariah, the poor thing. She'll see you tomorrow morning. You'll love her."

"What do you mean, society pariah?" I asked. I was sipping a Diet Coke in Harry's office. August had an iced tea. My face felt pink from our lunchtime sun.

Harry fired up his desktop computer, clicked on the keys, then turned the flat-screen monitor so we could see.

"Miriam Rose," he said. "On her wedding day. *New York Times* archive photo."

I held my breath. The picture was black-and-white,

but I had truly never seen a more beautiful woman in my entire life. She reminded me of an old-time movie star. Her Grace Kelly ash-blond hair was swept up into a chignon, and her neck was long and graceful. The intricate lace wedding gown fit her close, narrowing to a tiny waist then sweeping out into a cathedral train. Her hands resembled a porcelain doll's, her lips, a perfect rosebud, her cheekbones stretching up to pale eyes.

"She's gorgeous," I said.

"And she was married to Rose for years. She apparently turned a blind eye to his extramarital escapades and the fact that he was known as an emotional bully. But there was some sort of 'last straw' a couple of years ago, and they got divorced. He pretty much slashed and burned her life. Destroyed her. Fought her tooth and nail in the courtroom, and made sure that all their friends—and their two children—turned their backs on her."

"How could they do that, if they were really her friends? Her children?"

"He had the Rose name. The family fortune. Trusts. Art. Homes in London, Geneva, Los Angeles, and three places in New York City alone. He owned their world. All of it. She was penniless when he married her. It was rather scandalous at the time." He clicked some more keys, and I saw his cursor hover over a link. "If you read this article, a society reporter at the time was paid to 'invent' a little bit about her background. The real Miriam Rose came from nothing. And in this city, among members of that circle . . . money and power talks."

I leaned in closer to scan the article.

"Oh, and this one. Wait." Harry clicked and pressed the mouse button. A photo came up from the 1980s of her in an incredibly elegant ruby-red velvet gown. "This was her at a ball for the Metropolitan Museum of Art."

"I've seen that dress before . . . haven't I?" I asked.

"It's a Valentino. And remember that necklace Julia Roberts wore in *Pretty Woman?* The one she wore to the opera? It was modeled after Miriam's ruby and diamond set. Look at it. Remember?"

"I do!" I said. I leaned in and stared at her. "She's what? In her forties here?"

Harry mentally calculated. "I think so."

"She's still stunning."

Harry sighed. "Forty is *not* the kiss of death, you know."

I smiled at him. "Sorry, Crypt-Keeper."

"Don't make me kill you, favorite niece."

"*Only* niece," I corrected him. I looked back at

Miriam Rose in her gown. "She's smiling, but her eyes look sad. I feel sorry for her."

"Me, too," murmured August.

"I wonder," Harry said, clicking back to her wedding picture, "if she had any idea, as that beaming bride, what lay ahead."

"Do any of us?" August asked. "I didn't know yesterday that I was going to meet Calliope." He seemed to realize what he'd said, so hurriedly added, "Or be hunting for the author of a palimpsest."

I felt heat rush through my cheeks. Harry grinned. He was oh-so-proud of his matchmaking skills. In his circle of friends, he'd already had three weddings attributed to him, and he was godfather to one baby born of his setups.

August stood. "I've got to get back home. Need to get some groceries for my dad, especially if I'm going to be gone all day tomorrow." He looked at me. "What are you doing the rest of the day?"

I was about to say that I had to stay and work, when instead Harry blurted out, "Nothing."

I looked at my uncle, shocked.

"She's done for the day here. Off you go." He gestured like he was shooing a fly out of his office.

August grinned. "What do you say? If you come with me to the grocery store, I'll cook you dinner."

"Sure." I stood up. I wasn't going to argue about spending more time with August. "I'll see you later, Uncle Harry."

"Do you have cab money? I don't want you taking the subway late."

I nodded.

"All right, sweetie. Have fun."

I followed August out of Harry's office. When we left the auction house, we walked to the subway station. I slid my MetroCard through, and so did August. Then we descended the stairs. My calves were only too happy to remind me I had walked ninety flights of stairs already that day.

"How come you can go on the subway, but not in an elevator?"

"I like trains," he said. A train sped into the station, and its whoosh of hot air blew my hair around. August swept a piece from my face. In that minute, I didn't care that people were all around us hustling off the train and onto the train. He grabbed my hand and we boarded, but it was standing room only.

August held on to the overhead railing. He was so tall, it was effortless for him. I was packed in, squashed between him, a man in a suit with a briefcase, and an older woman wearing headphones and listening to her iPod. I could hear an old Beatles tune playing.

The subway car lurched as it pulled away. I tried to reach up to the railing, but I was a little too short to quite reach it. August instead clasped one of my arms, and pulled me to him to keep me balanced as the car rocked the way trains do. As the train sped through the dark tunnel, with every side-to-side motion, I felt how close he was, how pushed together we were. And I could hear him breathing heavily.

The car was hot, and I felt even warmer against him. At one point, the train lurched, and we were shoved together even closer, my chest pressed against his.

I shut my eyes for a minute, not sure whether I wanted him to kiss me so we could get that first kiss over, or whether I was terrified because I had never wanted someone to kiss me so much in my entire life. And terrified that I didn't have a whole lot of kissing experience. I kept my eyes closed until we came to our stop. Then I opened them. He was staring at me. "Come on," he whispered.

Holding my hand, we slid through the crowd and up the steps to the street above.

"One block this way to the grocery store."

Holding hands, I felt my chest pounding, and I was grateful when we got to the grocery store because it was something to do, something to distract me from how badly I wanted to kiss him and how scared I was. I had never felt scared like this before. Maybe nervous with a guy, first-date-jitters kind of thing (not that I'd had many first dates). But this was different.

August found us a cart, and he pushed it to the produce section, choosing fruits and vegetables.

"What do you say to steamed asparagus, seared ahi tuna, and couscous?" he asked, picking green asparagus, tall and tapered.

"I'd say my only attempt at cooking my entire life was my Easy-Bake Oven, so it sounds good."

He laughed. "An Easy-Bake Oven, huh? All right, maybe you can do dessert."

I shook my head. "I burned my Easy-Bake cakes. I can't believe you can really make a dinner like that." Uncle Harry believed in takeout, and Gabe was always at the theater. At home in Boston, I would either eat at my best friend's house, where her mother believes the Chinese restaurant around the corner is her personal chef, or, rarely, when he showed up, my dad and would I eat out at his country club. But most nights I lived on ramen and anything frozen that could be put on a cookie sheet in the oven, heated at 425 degrees, and called a meal.

"Well, my father obviously doesn't go out to restaurants, so I started cooking so that it was *like* eating out, only we were eating in. I was thirteen when I learned to make hollandaise."

"Impressive."

"Well, reserve judgment until after I've cooked for you. My couscous is occasionally a little rubbery."

We wandered the aisles, filling our cart with fresh vegetables, a loaf of bread, juice, and soda. He plucked a bouquet of fresh flowers from a bucket and handed them to me.

"For you."

I smelled the freesia. August wasn't like anyone I had ever met before. He was a lot more mature. He didn't seem interested in things typical guys were interested in. I didn't know what to think. Then again, I didn't really want to think—just to experience being with him.

He paid for the groceries, and we walked the four blocks to his house.

"Dad?" He called out when we entered.

"In here, August." I heard his father's voice from down the hall.

"I have Calliope with me."

I followed August into the kitchen, where he set down the groceries. Then we walked down the hall, and he poked his head into his father's office.

I stood to the side. His father smiled at us.

"I'm making tuna, asparagus . . . Give me a half hour or so, Dad."

His father waved his hands. "No. I'm so sorry I didn't tell you. I didn't know how late you would be. I already made myself a sandwich and ate at my desk. You cook for Calliope."

"You sure?"

"Of course."

"Okay. See you later."

August started back toward the kitchen. I smiled and waved my hand at Professor Sokolov. He winked at me and beamed. I looked on his desk. No plate—he hadn't eaten. He was as obvious as Uncle Harry with this matchmaking bit.

In the kitchen August turned on a Bose SoundDock with an iPod placed in it. He touched the screen and found what he was looking for. Norah Jones's dreamy voice floated out from the speakers.

August put some of the groceries away. Then he started pulling out pans.

"Can I help?"

"Nope. You already told me you can't cook. I'm not letting you *near* my pans," he teased.

"Then I'll just watch," I pretend-pouted and moved to the other side of the granite counter.

"You'll be able to see better over here."

"I can see standing over here," I said.

"But I can't smell your perfume from over there."

He turned and got me a small vase for the flowers he had bought me. And then he cooked. I had never really noticed a guy's hands before, but I liked watching him chopping parsley and garlic with the knife, the way his fingers curled. He hands looked strong and very masculine.

Soon, the stovetop was sizzling, and steam was rising from the asparagus. August pulled out a pitcher of water with lemon slices floating in it and walked out the kitchen's back door to his garden. He stepped in and out a few times, carrying things, and I carried a couple of bowls to help him.

When I walked out into the garden, I felt my body instantly relax. The koi pond gurgled; the birds twittered. Strung along the fence were twinkling white lights. It wasn't dark yet—not in summer—but I knew, come nightfall, the garden had to be absolutely enchanting.

I glanced at the table August had been setting. It was a simple wrought-iron table-and-chair set. He had covered the table with a white linen tablecloth and candles.

"Sit down," he said. "I'll be back with our plates in a minute."

He returned with our dinner. Everything was perfect—even his couscous. And it was an awful lot like eating out at a restaurant. I gave him a lot of credit for adapting to his father's eccentricities.

He asked me, "How did you get the name Calliope?"

"My mother was a singer, and the name is from a daughter of Zeus. It means 'beautiful voice.' I think she hoped I could sing, too. But if you heard my singing voice . . . I can tell you that my name doesn't suit me, put it that way. I'm no Norah Jones. And how did you get the name August? Your birthday?"

He nodded. "Born in August, and my mother's favorite sculptor was Auguste Rodin."

We talked all through supper, about our families and about music. About everything and nothing all at once. When supper was finished, I could see the sky turning gray with a wash of pink. A summer sky perfect for how I felt.

August stood. "Come on, let's feed the koi."

We walked to the koi pond. Fat goldfish kissed the surface, waiting for their dinner. We fed them, watching them flip onto their sides in a dance for the most pellets of food. Then we sat on a bench next to the pond, the water gurgling and peaceful.

"Do you think Miriam Rose will lead us to A.?"

He shrugged and took my hand, tracing my palm with his index finger. Even though it was hot out, I shivered.

"I've learned that just when you think you have something all figured out . . . there's another layer to it," he said.

He kept tracing my palm, and then we just sat in the quiet of his garden, until the sun set and the garden was illuminated by the white twinkling lights, and the birds had quieted in their nests. Until it felt like we were the only two people in the entire world.

6

Storms rage. Passions thunder. —A.

August insisted on coming all the way home with me, in the cab, making sure I was safely back at Uncle Harry's apartment. I waved good-bye, and as I watched the cab pull away with him in the backseat, headed to his own house, I thought my insides would spill into the street. He was gone for a minute, and it felt like forever.

Upstairs, Uncle Harry waited, glass of red wine in his hand, jazz on the stereo. It was his and Gabe's nightly tradition. Uncle Harry waited until Gabe got home, then they shared a glass of wine, listened to Herbie Hancock or John Coltrane or Miles Davis, and talked about their day.

"Calliope," Uncle Harry said with a smile, "tell me the dress from Barney's and my matchmaking skills were a success. Did you have a nice time?"

I sighed happily, not sure of what to say. Instead,

I blurted out, "He's perfect, Harry. Absolutely perfect."

"Better than that guy you were dating sophomore year ... the one who got into Boston College on a lacrosse scholarship. What was his name?"

"You know his name is Charlie." I shook my head. "You just never liked him."

"And was I *wrong?*"

"You're going to make me say it, aren't you, Crypt-Keeper?"

"Ouch." He pretended to pull an invisible knife from his chest. "She plays the age card yet again. But yes, I am going to make you say it."

I pretend-gritted my teeth. "You were *right* about Charlie. That was something untrustworthy about him. Like the fact that he was cheating on me."

"And I said, take a little time to get over it, but then go right out there and find someone as special as you are. But you took a 'little time' and stretched it into all of junior year. So I had to take matters into my own hands."

"I just didn't like anyone this year. My school's so small. Most of the guys seem more like ... I don't know, pesky brothers. We know each other so well. But August ... no one can be *that* cute *and* that smart *and* that nice. No one."

"Oh yes, he can. I've known him and his father a long time. Callie, it's not just *any boy* I'd introduce you to. Like the Meyers' son, down the hall? He's not good enough for you by a long shot. He went in the rejection pile right away."

"He's just creepy."

"Right. And you know Georgina, in the Appraisal Department at the auction house? She's shown me her son's picture a hundred times, trying to get me to fix you two up. But I happen to know from Stella in research that he's trouble with a capital T. Flunked out of two private schools already."

"Now you're being a gossip," I teased him.

"Only where you're concerned. But August... he's a straight-A student, good-looking, takes compassionate care of his father, is smart and courteous. He's the type of guy I want for you. So once again. I was—what did you say?"

"Old."

"No, after that."

"Right." I yawned. "You were right. And now, I better go to bed. He and I have to leave really early to get out to Miriam Rose's—we have to catch a ferry."

"All right, sweetie." He sipped his wine. "And Callie..."

"Yeah?"

"You *deserve* to be happy. Remember that."

"Okay. Thanks."

"And it's okay to have fun, to do something just for the sheer joy of it, not for how it looks on your Harvard application."

I nodded and walked to him to kiss him good night. "Thanks, Crypt-Keeper," I whispered.

"Love you."

"Love you, too." In my room, I changed into a T-shirt and boy shorts and flicked on the television. I don't think I saw ten minutes of a *Law & Order* rerun before I was fast asleep.

Sometime in the night, I had a dream that I was standing inside a castle. At least I thought it was a castle. And I was searching for something, going from room to room. Or I was running from something or someone. I could hear a voice. I was frightened. The voice was begging me to run, *run*! And I thought it was August's voice, but it wasn't August's voice. All I know was I woke up, my blankets tangled around me as if I had been thrashing around in my bed. And at the precise moment I woke up—3:07 A.M., since I looked at the clock—my cell phone dinged.

I had a text message. From August. At 3:07.

MISS U

I texted back.

ME 2

I wasn't sure how I could miss someone I'd just seen that night, someone I'd just met not forty-eight hours before, but I did. My cell phone dinged again.

Can't wait until tomorrow. Can't sleep.

I smiled and texted back.

I just woke up. Weird dream.

Then his turn...

What was it about?

I texted back.

Not really sure.

I sent the message and punched my pillow.

Go back to sleep. See U tomorrow. Sweet dreams, angel!

Morning arrived gray and dreary, an ominous sky. And while I didn't feel dreary, I was tired.

I sat up and ran my hands through my hair. Aggie had come in during the night and was now purring contentedly on my pillow, as peaceful as I wish my own sleep had been.

I climbed out of bed and looked in the mirror. Concealer was definitely in order.

I went into the bathroom and showered. I put on makeup, and dressed in nice jeans and a camisole, with a white cardigan over it. After packing a purse with my iPhone, wallet, lip gloss, and a brush, I walked out to the kitchen. Gabe was eating standing up at the counter—his usual of an English muffin slathered in honey and butter.

"I hear love is in the air," he said, greeting me and handing me a cup of coffee in my favorite mug.

"Maybe." I tried to play it cool.

"I see it in your eyes."

"My eyes say I have circles under them and got no sleep."

"That's what love is, at first. No one sleeps when

they're first in love. They usually don't eat, either. And the brain turns to mush."

"Well, I definitely can't sleep. And I'm not hungry." I sipped my coffee. "And my brain would definitely be mush without caffeine."

"You and your uncle. It's your life juice."

"I don't understand how you can drink tea."

"It's so much healthier. But enough about me! I want to hear about loverboy. Harry's been wanting to play matchmaker for a while now. Did you know he set up Leon and James? They're on their second anniversary. And Liz—my old vocal coach—and Darius. And my sister, Bridget, and her new boyfriend, Stuart. He's a regular eHarmony. And this manuscript . . . maybe it was fate. He wanted to play matchmaker, and the manuscript made it easy."

"What's that I hear about matchmaker?" Harry walked in and leaned down to kiss me on the top of my head, then pecked Gabe on the cheek. He looked at his watch. "You ready, Callie? Where are you meeting August?"

"He's coming here."

I sipped my coffee, refilled it, and a few minutes later, the concierge buzzed up that August was in the lobby. My heart started pounding—and not because I was hyped up on caffeine. "How do I look?"

"Like a dream. Now go . . . and call me after you meet with Miriam."

I grabbed my bag and hurriedly left, willing the elevator to go faster. Finally, the doors opened in the lobby.

Part of me, riding down in the elevator, wondered if I had just created August out of thin air. Made up how great he was. But then he turned around, and I saw him and wanted to run to him. He walked over and gave me a hug.

"Ready to go chasing the mystery of A.?"

"Yeah." I smiled, pulled away, and took his hand. We rode a subway and then took a train out to Long Island. From there, we made our way to the ferry.

Wind was whipping the Long Island Sound into frothy, white-capped beauty. The wind blew salt water onto my face, and my hair flew wildly, pieces slapping against my cheeks and eyes.

"Some storm coming," I said to him, raising my voice to be heard.

He nodded and stood beside me, watching as the wide ferry docked. It rocked from side to side, looking more and more like a toy boat bobbing in a bathtub.

We boarded with just a handful of people. We climbed down below deck and chose two seats. I shivered, and he wrapped an arm around me.

"I didn't expect the weather to be like this," I said.

"Me, either. I didn't look at the weather report." He squinted as he scanned the horizon outside the window. A bolt of lightning jaggedly shot across the sky.

The ferry jerked as it pulled away from the dock. It swayed from side to side, the waves tossing her. I tried to focus on the cloud-shrouded horizon to keep from feeling seasick. I wanted my feet on the ground before I turned green. When we finally docked, the ferry captain came out of the wheelhouse and said, "Might be the last ride of the day."

I looked at August, a worried expression on my face. "What if we can't get back?"

He shrugged. "We'll swim."

I rolled my eyes. "Now, why didn't I think of that?"

"Look, I don't know, but we didn't come this far not to see Miriam Rose. Maybe it'll clear in the afternoon."

According to my iPhone's Google map, we could walk to Miriam's house from the ferry. We found the shore drive, and read street addresses on the beach houses, their shingles weathered and worn to a gray-brown Cape-Cod–looking appearance.

We found Miriam's house, nestled down close to the beach and nearly hidden by natural vegetation, scrubby-looking sumac and bushes and tall bursts of reedy grasses. As we descended her drive, the mist picked up to a full-blown rainstorm, with huge drops bombarding us in earnest.

We half jogged to her door, ringing the bell as icy rain pelted us.

A dog barked loudly, and the door opened. A big golden retriever wagged its tail and pushed its nose toward us in greeting. Behind the dog stood Miriam, older but just as beautiful as her wedding-day picture. "Honi," she commanded, "move aside." She patted her dog at the same time as she pushed it out of our way. "I just spoke with Harry. You poor angels," she murmured. "I didn't think you would try to come out given the weather report. Come on in, hurry."

We stepped inside her beach house, and I saw I was dripping water on her sleek slate floors, forming a puddle.

"I'm so sorry," I said, shivering slightly and pulling my shoulders up as if by holding very still I could keep from dripping.

"Let me go get you towels. What a squall!" She looked out the bank of windows that rose, floor to ceiling, along the front of the house in the living room. Rain lashed at the panes in sheets. "I usually love a good storm—but not being out in one."

I glanced at August and felt my insides churn. Dripping wet, he was even sexier. *How was that possible?!* When Miriam disappeared, the dog followed her. August raised an eyebrow playfully. "You know I can see through your shirt," he whispered.

I looked down, aware that white was the worst possible choice today. "Yeah . . . and I'm sure I look like a drowned rat."

"No," he whispered. "You look beautiful."

My teeth chattered, and I was certain my lips were blue.

Miriam returned with two huge, plush towels and two oversize hooded sweatshirts.

"Here. The bathroom is over there. You can at least change into these sweatshirts. In the rain, we weren't properly introduced. I'm Miriam . . . and I know from Harry that you are Calliope and August." We shook hands. "And this oversize and over-eager puppy is Honi." Her dog barked as if it understood her.

I apologized again for the rain on her floor as we started drying off as best we could.

"I live at the beach. Believe me, sand and water on my floors are a way of life. And dog hair."

I dried my hair with the towel and went into the bathroom to change into the sweatshirt.

When I came out, August had already slipped his sweatshirt on.

"How about some hot tea?" Miriam suggested.

I nodded gratefully, and the two of us followed her into the kitchen.

"Sit down—don't worry about the chairs," she said. "Everything in this house is meant to be sat on with wet bathing suits or walked on with sandy sneakers. It's a different life from my old one in the city."

August and I sat in chairs around the oak farm table that dominated the kitchen. She turned to put the kettle on, and I looked around. The cabinets were antique-looking, some with glass fronts. In them stood an array of brightly colored plates and goblets, along with seashells and jars filled with bits of sea glass. It was nothing like her son's cold apartment.

Miriam padded over to the table and set down cups and saucers, along with a jar of honey, a sugar bowl, and a small tin containing different types of tea. She wore pale denim capris and a white Oxford-cloth shirt. She wore no jewelry except for an antique-looking locket hanging from a chain around her neck. Her hair, which had been pale blond in the pictures, was now blond mixed with strands of silver. It fell to her shoulders, and it seemed to curl naturally into soft waves.

"Calliope, you're Harry's niece?"

"Yes, ma'am."

"Call me Miriam. Do you two take milk with your tea? Or cream? I even have soy milk."

"I just take honey," I said.

"Just sugar for me," August replied.

"All right then." She turned to open a pantry door. "I have tea biscuits. Now where are they? Oh . . . here."

She emerged from the pantry with a box of biscuits, which she opened and arranged on a porcelain plate painted with violets along the edges.

She sat down at the table. "I talked to Harry briefly, but he didn't tell me anything. This is about the book, isn't it?"

August nodded. "Yes."

"The Book of Hours?"

"Yes," I said softly.

Her face was unlined, and her cheekbones and graceful neck made her look much younger than what August and I had calculated her to be—seventy. Her eyes sparkled when she spoke of the book.

"You've seen it?" she asked hopefully, twisting her long fingers around a cloth napkin she'd put beside her plate.

I nodded.

She dropped the cloth and clasped her hands to her breast. "I thought . . ." Then she put her face in her hands and softly cried.

August and I exchanged glances. He stood and put a hand on her shoulder. "We didn't mean to upset you. Your former butler told us to call. He said you would want to know."

She stared up at August gratefully, "No, you don't understand. These are happy tears. I've waited years to know my book, the Book of Hours, the book of A., was safe."

My heart pounded. Now I understood how Uncle Harry and Dr. Sokolov felt. It really was like playing detective.

"It's safe," I said softly. "I've *seen* it. We both have."

She smiled. "You probably think I'm foolish. It's a book. Just a book. But A. . . . he had a way of making me believe in love."

7

Midnight greets my dreams of her.

—A.

The teakettle whistled, and, wiping her eyes, Miriam went to the stove and filled our cups with boiling water. When she sat down again, she said, simply, "I suppose you've come all this way in this terrible storm to hear the story."

We nodded in unison. I was growing more and more devoted to the book. To A. And to August.

"Well," Miriam sighed, stirring her tea, "then it's just as well the storm is here. Might as well settle in and tell you."

August sipped his tea, then said, "Thank you. We really do want to know. Did you know it was a palimpsest? You must have, because you know about A."

"I did know. Though not at first."

"You understand how rare it is, I guess. A palimpsest."

"Yes, I do. And how it came to me . . . I suppose it starts all the way back. To my wedding. My honeymoon. And shortly after."

"We saw your wedding picture on the Internet," I said.

She smiled ruefully. "Such a naïve young girl, I was. My husband spotted me working in Wanamaker's. They don't even *have* Wanamaker's anymore. But it was an incredible store back then. I worked at the scarf and glove counter, and this elegant man—older than I was—came in wanting a pair of leather gloves. I remember specifically. He wanted kid leather, soft, in a deep brown."

She laughed quietly. "Like any impressionable girl with no money and big dreams, I was swept off my feet. But Thomas A. Rose wasn't just any man. He was old money. Ruthless money. I didn't know what I was getting into. Not at all. I only knew that suddenly, I was going to the theater and the ballet, was being invited to balls, and was dressing in couture. Our wedding was *the* social event of the year, including a fake biography for me and my parents, which implied my mother and father were of European royalty. Nothing could have been further from the truth. My father was a tailor. But his impeccable suits and elegant manners helped us carry off the deception. However, people still whispered about me behind my back."

Miriam was so nice. I hated the idea of people gossiping about her. There was a "mean girls" pack at my school, and I couldn't stand the way they were nice to people's faces but then turned right around and said the ugliest thing. "I'm sorry. They were just jealous, I bet."

"Maybe. They said I was a showgirl, which was . . . well, in *those* days it implied I was a woman of ill repute. But I held my head high, and after a time the rumors stopped."

I held on to my teacup, afraid to breathe. Afraid to interrupt her.

"Of course, I think Thomas just wanted to *acquire* me, as one acquires a thoroughbred horse. For some time, he spoiled me. I indeed had horses out on our Long Island estate. We had dozens of them and a full-time trainer. I had an apartment on Park Avenue, with accounts at every store a woman could possibly care to spend money at." She laughed.

"I had jewelry, most of which sits in a box upstairs. I had a famous ruby necklace."

"We saw it in a picture," I said.

"Yes. *That one* I sold at Christie's. I just have no occasion or reason to wear something like that. But I had, most of all, unending time on my hands."

"You must have been bored," August said.

"Oh, I was. Hopelessly bored. Even when I was just a glove and scarf clerk, I read voraciously. I thirsted for knowledge. I wanted someday to go to college, but once I met Thomas, he thought that was out of the question. Whatever for, he would ask me?" She stopped.

"Miriam, what is it?" August asked softly.

"I really *must* be very lonely, with only my dog for companionship. Here I am blathering on to you two, when you really just want to know about the book."

"No, no!" I said right away. "Really, tell us the whole story." I was fascinated—her life, it was like a movie, only real.

"Anyway, on our honeymoon, we had traveled to Europe, and for the first time, I saw convents and cathedrals, museums that weren't just housing old paintings, but were older than the paintings themselves. I loved it. And by the time I was home and ensconced on the boards of various museums, and largely ignored by my husband, I wanted to do something more than be a lady of leisure."

"What did your husband say?" I asked.

"Well, I later found out that he had never stopped frequenting some . . . lady friends. Never. So I think he was happy to have that beautiful doll—the perfectly clothed little creature in his tower—and that she had something to do other than question him about his whereabouts after work."

I wondered about my dad and mom. She was beautiful, and Uncle Harry said she had hated some of my father's expectations of her as the wife of a powerful attorney. And then there was the endless parade of girlfriends since she died.

A crack of lightning illuminated the sky outside. It sounded like it was right above us.

Miriam glanced heavenward. "Makes you wonder if A. doesn't want his story told." She looked at me and winked.

"You said 'he,'" August said. "You know A. is a he?" He gave me a look that said, *I told you so*.

"Yes. And even if he's a little upset, I'll tell the story anyway. Maybe he's impatient! Maybe he wants it told right now. I happened to be acquiring art for our summer home—a huge mansion out here on Long Island that Thomas still owns. Well, now my son own it," she corrected herself. "It's over in the Hamptons. Maybe a half mile from Billy Joel's place. Anyway, Thomas had been rather impressed that three paintings I asked him to purchase tripled in value rather quickly. So he allowed me to go to art auctions on my own." She smiled ruefully. "Not truly alone, mind you. I attended with a gentleman from his accounting firm, who authorized my purchases. But the decisions were my own. Soon, we had one of the most talked-about collections in all of New York. Thomas enjoyed being talked about. He enjoyed the prestige our collection afforded him. And it was on one of my hunts that I saw the auction of my first illuminated manuscripts."

"That's what Uncle Harry does," I said. "Did you meet him then?"

She laughed. "Your uncle Harry isn't quite that old, dear. But like your Harry I was completely infatuated with illuminated manuscripts. They're extraordinary, really. Did you know that monks originally created many of them, but as the Middle Ages wore on, many of the painters were women, particularly in Paris? That appealed to me. I guess I was developing a new dream of freedom, and the manuscripts represented that to me. They were exquisite."

I looked over at August. "I didn't know that the painters were women. Did you?"

August nodded then turned back to Miriam. "And you were interested in the Gothic period, right?"

My eyes widened. Uncle Harry was right. August was really, really smart.

She nodded. "Wise, my dear August. You know your subject matter. Yes. Like many collectors, I wanted a collection that was specialized, and so the Gothic period became my area of expertise. And as Thomas and I led increasingly separate lives, it seemed to be with an understanding that I didn't ask about his young friends. And he opened his checkbook for my collection."

I finished sipping the last of my tea. Miriam noticed and said, "Come, let's go to the living room. There's a beautiful view of the water; even in this storm, it'll be lovely. We can talk more there, and I can show you my photos of the hunt for the Book of Hours."

She stood, and August and I followed her. He brushed his hand against mine as we walked, and I ached to hold it.

Her living room was decorated with overstuffed chairs covered in Shabby Chic–type fabrics. The coffee table and end tables were piled high with books, and mason jars were filled with shells, sand, starfish, and sea glass—there was even one jar with old buttons and one with Scrabble letter tiles.

It was a very big room, but the way she had arranged the furniture and the lamps, and even the framed prints of beach scenes on the walls, made it seem cozy. August and I sat on the long sofa, and she sat on a large chaise lounge covered with pillows next to us. I shivered slightly; the soaking we'd had must have chilled me more than I knew.

"Here, Calliope." She leaped up and handed me a thick quilt that had been folded on an ottoman. "You must be freezing. And I know just the thing." She walked over to a pass-through glass and white-stone fireplace, pressed a button, and a gas fire sprang to life, blue and white flames licking ceramic logs.

I pulled the quilt up and spread it over my legs. She returned to her chaise and pulled a heavy scrapbook from the end table next to it. She set it on her lap and inhaled as if contemplating whether or not even to open it.

"I haven't looked inside this scrapbook since I moved here. Maybe it hurt too much." She opened the cover.

"It's full of memories of the hunt for the book. I first heard about this particular illuminated manuscript while researching the love story of Heloise and Abelard."

"Who were they?" I asked.

She smiled at me. "Probably two of the world's most infamous star-crossed lovers. Tragic figures. Hopelessly intellectual. Somewhat forgotten, I suppose. But not by everyone."

I curled my knees up under me. August moved his hand to rest on my thigh. I put my hand on his.

"Heloise was born in 1101, and she was a brilliant young girl. She was the ward of her uncle, Fulbert, who was a canon in the church. Recognizing her gifted mind, he allowed her to be schooled—something quite rare for the time. You can understand why her story then fascinated me. I saw myself in Heloise. I was a young girl hungering for education in books and art. She was, too. I just . . . have you ever related to someone from history?"

I nodded. "I went through a Madame Curie phase in fourth grade. I had a microscope and slides—my bathroom was my lab."

August smiled at me. "That is really cute! I went through a major Charles Darwin phase in first grade—that was the start of my finch collection. I wanted to sail to the Galápagos."

Miriam nodded. "So you do understand. For me, it was Heloise. And I was well past elementary school," she joked.

"Heloise wasn't known as the most beautiful girl, but she was very smart. She wrote beautifully, was a scholar of Latin and Greek. Even Hebrew. And Fulbert allowed her to be tutored by Peter Abelard, himself a *brilliant* man. He was of noble birth and could have lived in great wealth, but chose philosophy and a more austere, scholarly life. He found her mind extraordinary. They fell in love, pupil and tutor. And a torrid affair blossomed."

I glanced at August. He was as riveted by Miriam's story as I was.

"What Peter loved most was her mind. And here I was, loved for my beauty by my husband, but ignored for my mind. I had dreams of a love like that. A soul mate." I understood what she meant. Wanting a soul mate, someone who understood you, all of you. I caught August's eye, then turned away.

"They loved each other madly, and Heloise became pregnant. The very idea was scandalous. She bore him a son. And then in Shakespearean-tragedy fashion, she was forced to enter a convent."

August said, "It's got all the elements of a classic tragic love story."

"Oh, but there is so much more," Miriam said. "She and Peter had secretly married, and when Fulbert found out . . . Well, he had men loyal to him severely beat and then castrate Peter Abelard."

I covered my mouth with a gasp. "No!"

Miriam nodded. "I know. A horrible tragedy. And all true."

"What did they do?" I asked, now leaning forward. I hadn't realized it, but I was gripping August's hand.

"They didn't correspond for some time afterward. Peter, as is understandable, felt very sorry for himself. He withdrew from life."

"Withdrew?" I asked.

"He became a hermit. He would see or speak to absolutely no one. Eventually, Heloise, who years later had risen to head her convent and was now an abbess . . . she chastised him. She took him to task. It's funny—she basically was the stronger person. She told him he needed to stop his self-pity. And so began a series of letters between them—theological in nature, philosophical. The meeting of the minds was still present, was still palpable between them, even after all that happened. At first, I think she hoped to rekindle their great love affair—even after all that time, he was her one true heart. But if she could not have him as her love, then she was determined to have his mind—to be his confidante, and best friend, his intellectual equal."

"So A. is Abelard? Is that what you think?" August asked. "Because that would be incredible."

She smiled. "No, my dears. I believe A. is an even better find. One that would make history."

"Who then?"

"Heloise and Abelard's son. *Astrolabe.*"

8

Who is this ghost before me? —A.

"Their son?" I asked. I could hardly imagine.

She nodded. "Here's where my journey grows increasingly complicated." She stood and crossed over to the couch, sat next to us, and spread the scrapbook open on her lap.

"No one knows what happened to Astrolabe. This poor, innocent child, born into a secret marriage under tragic circumstances. His very existence caused his own father to be brutalized. Supposedly, Peter Abelard took him to his sister to be adopted. He was raised with his aunt instead of his parents as would be right. Raised separated from his mother. But we know little of what happened to him. One theory is he also went into the church. There's a reference to him as Venerable, later on, which would support that. But it's unclear."

"What about their letters? Did they ever discuss

him?" I asked, incredulous that they could have forgotten their love child.

"Peter makes a reference to him in a single line or two. That, because it is important to *her*, he would attempt to secure a position for Astrolabe in the religious life. But beyond that, the poor little boy is a ghost."

"So why do you think it's Astrolabe who wrote those words?" I asked. "Why him and not Peter. Or someone else? Why this *one* person in history?" I was hooked. Hooked on the story, hooked on the hunt, on the ghost of A. and the secret manuscript. I couldn't remember the last time I'd felt so thrilled, so excited. Hunting through history like this wasn't like anything I had ever done before—it was like being a treasure hunter and a detective all in one.

She touched the corner of one of the scrapbook pages. "I had heard whisperings of some artifacts from Heloise. But you have to understand, because she and Peter Abelard were so famous, there is much myth surrounding them that is presented as fact. For instance, some say they are buried together at the Père-Lachaise Cemetery in Paris. Others are not so sure and think perhaps it's a mere monument. A statue with no remains." She flipped through the scrapbook and held a page up to us. "Here's a picture of their supposed crypt."

I looked down at the monument and touched the picture. Two stone figures lay faceup, next to each other, hands folded in prayer, beneath an open-walled stone pergola. Her face was serene, his solemn.

"It's beautiful," I whispered. "Do you think they are there? That they are really side by side, forever?" There was something tragic and romantic about the idea, the two of them still entwined.

She smiled at me. "I like to think so, Calliope. I like to think that despite what the world did to them, tearing them apart, confining her in a convent, ripping her child from her arms, perhaps, that in the end, they sleep, side by side. Really at rest. Really at peace. Forever and ever."

The cemetery look ancient, and the stone was gray with age, lichen-covered in spots, chiseled and beautifully elegant. The pergola rose to a point, and light streamed in on four sides.

"I was on the hunt—an adventure. And I was captivated, addicted to it. The hunt was all I thought about. I was entranced." She smiled at both of us. "And judging by your faces, you are too. Are you not?"

August grinned. "I've been around manuscripts my whole life—and Miriam? This is the best hunt yet."

I nodded. "Tell us the rest. *Please.*"

"An antiquarian in Paris had heard rumors of a Book of Hours, that perhaps had belonged to Heloise. And even though there was little way to confirm it for sure, I was certain I wanted to own it, or at least *see* it. I can't explain it, but Heloise represented my true awakening."

She turned the page. Photos of sketches of Heloise as she is thought to have looked and copies of her letters to Peter Abelard filled the scrapbook.

Then there was a picture of a man. "This is Etienne Dupont," she said.

I looked down. An older gentleman with an elegant silver mustache and a dimple in his chin stood facing the camera. His eyes were deep blue, and he was grinning like a mischievous child. I looked over at Miriam. She was blushing.

"To Etienne, the hunt was just as exciting. I flew to Paris. We tracked down every lead, followed every rumor. I explained it to Thomas as the find of a lifetime. Priceless. Say 'priceless' to Thomas, and there was no expense too high. No stone to leave unturned. But I didn't care about how much the manuscript was worth. I cared about Heloise, about the tragic love story. About finding out who these people in history really were."

I nodded. I couldn't explain it, but from the moment I saw the secret writing, I was certain A. had something important to say.

Miriam continued. "Then we met an old man whose family had passed down the Book of Hours for generations and generations. They had preserved it perfectly, but told no one."

"Was it the Book of Hours? That Harry has?"

She nodded. "Etienne made arrangements for a private sale. I told my husband it would be the cornerstone of our collection. I was certain there was something extraordinary about it."

"And?" August was hanging on her every word.

"And I brought it home. But I had no idea. None. That it was a palimpsest. Even a well-preserved manuscript of this sort is extremely rare and extraordinary, as I'm sure you know, August. I can't tell you the thrill I felt to see it. Like all illuminated manuscripts, yes, the gilt edges of the pages were beautiful, the paintings detailed. And it was fragile. Incredibly so. But I was certain it had an association with Heloise and Abelard. I *felt* it. In my soul. Does that make sense?"

"It does," I whispered.

"I brought it home. By private jet. Afterward, after it was safely in New York, I discovered it was a palimpsest. Once I was home, I also received a handwritten letter from Etienne."

She bit her lip. "He professed . . . his love for me. Told me it was all right if I didn't feel the same, but that he was certain our shared love of Heloise, of the book, was more than coincidence." She swallowed.

"Was it?" I thought of the icy apartment, of her son so callously selling what she clearly loved and treasured for more than its dollar amount.

"I couldn't believe that at my age, I had found what had eluded me all my life. A soul mate."

"Oh, Miriam," I said. I clasped her hand, feeling a bursting inside of me at the thought that such a sweet person had found true love. But then I remembered that she had lost everything, been cast out of New York society. So where did Miriam's story really end?

She shook her head. "By then, my husband's paramours were in their late twenties—younger and younger. They were indiscreet. They occasionally even showed up at the same parties that we did. One even came to the apartment, asking him for a credit card so she could purchase clothes. I begged him to stop humiliating me. I didn't want to end my marriage, if only because I did recall a time when I thought my husband loved me. Treasured me like a delicate rose. That was his little name for me. The Rose's rose."

She wiped at her eye. "But he wouldn't listen. And then, when he saw how I told the story of the book, he became suspicious. He found Etienne's letter. I had hidden it, not yet sure of my reply, of what to say. Thomas found it among my jewelry, folded into the lining of my jewelry box. He was furious. Said that I had made him a cuckolded man."

"But . . . had . . . you and Etienne even . . ." I struggled to find the words, not even sure if I should ask. It seemed impolite.

"No," she said ruefully. "To be honest, I wish I had. But no. However, my husband had a new passion— to destroy me. He reminded me that I had come from nothing, and he would return me to nothing."

"But you were married a long time. Had children together. And *you* were the wronged one. All those affairs. Couldn't you fight back?" I asked. I couldn't believe the way he had treated her.

She looked to August and then to me. "So young. Full of spirit. I see it in both of you. It's not so simple at my age. To let my whole world be dragged through the mud? All I had built, my collection split up, destroyed. I tried to keep things dignified. To simply settle it. That was my way."

I saw her whole expression change, like the sky outside. Her eyes clouded.

"I had a very good legal team, and I refused to sink to his level. I never once spoke to the press. But it didn't matter. He hid assets. He fought me on every point. He told my son and daughter that they would be written out of his will unless they sided with him. My daughter was always very fragile in some ways. When she was a teenager and in her early twenties, she had dabbled in drugs, and then she married a very shallow man who was only too happy to live off of her allowance. She needed her father's money. And my son, well, you met him yourself." She shook her head. "Thomas threatened to pull funding from any charity that left me on their board. I had friends on those boards, and they didn't want to hurt me. I resigned, rather than let the charities suffer. My friends, my children, my home, they were all gone."

My throat was dry. How could he do that to her? My heart pounded with anger, but it ached for Miriam at the same time.

"Finally, he offered a large sum. My lawyers said I could have gotten far more in court, but I had already lost everything. And so I accepted the offer. Even though to him it was nothing, believe me, it was more money than I could hope to spend in five lifetimes. I accepted it to be done, to have it finally be over."

"That was it?" I asked incredulously. "You settled, Miriam?"

"Yes, for tens of millions of dollars and my dignity. I came out here and bought this house. That was part of the agreement. He was to buy me a house of my own choosing. I didn't want some ostentatious mansion. I wanted peace. I didn't bring so much as a stick of furniture here. It was a new life. And when I accepted this settlement, I had his *word* that the collection would not be sold—that the book would not be sold. He swore to me."

"And did he honor that?" August asked.

"It wasn't in writing. He wouldn't agree to put it in writing. But he swore to it. Once, after a cocktail or two, he had admitted to dozens of affairs—even confessing that he had brought home women to sleep in our own marital bed! And he agreed that this one kindness he would show me. He kept his word. For a time. Then when he died, his will left the collection to my son, with the express instructions it be auctioned. The entire thing. Split up. With the proceeds to be split fifty-fifty between his mistress and my son."

I fell back against the couch. "Can't you call your son? Reason with him?"

She laughed derisively. "Have you *met* my son?"

"Contest the will then. Fight this, Miriam. Please," August said.

"Very little chance of that, dear. He knew what he was doing—he was of sound mind. It was a private promise; it wasn't in writing. There's nothing to be done. It was his last act to destroy me. From beyond the grave."

"But," I sputtered. "But ... now what? You *can't* let the book go to someone who doesn't care about Heloise. Couldn't you bid on it? Get it back?"

"I could. But once the auction world knows it's a palimpsest, even my money will be no match for others who want to acquire it. And worse, my son could always decide to withhold it from auction, wait until after I'm gone and then auction it."

"But why would your son do that?" I asked. "You didn't do anything to him."

"Maybe I did." She smiled ruefully. "I couldn't protect him from his father's plans for him. He expected so much of James. He was a rather cold and ruthless father. And all my interventions came to naught."

I thought of my father's plans for me. I wondered if my mother hadn't died of cancer, whether she would have been able to protect me from his controlling ways.

"Worst of all, I wasn't able to find any hard proof that the book belonged to Astrolabe before the divorce proceedings started. I'd never been able to prove that my suspicions were correct."

"Miriam," I asked, "do you feel sure the book belonged to Astrolabe?"

"I do. There are words that speak of his parents' love affair, of their near destruction of each other. And they very nearly did destroy each other until they found the intellectual side to their relationship again in later life. After the sexual side had been stolen from them by Fulbert. And now no one will ever know that it's Astrolabe's book."

"We know. And we can get the proof," August said, a passion in his voice. "We can trace the history."

"And you could help us, Miriam," I chimed in.

She seemed to brighten. "Well . . . the obvious place to start would be with Etienne, but I am certain he has never forgiven me for not writing back."

"You never did?" August asked.

"No. What could I say?"

"But we have to try, Miriam. How can we get in touch with Etienne?" August asked.

"He lives in Paris. He knows the original bookseller, the original owner's family. Or, he did. It's been a few years."

"Then we have to go to Paris," August said firmly.

I stared at him. Paris. Us? "Yes!" I practically squealed. More than anything I wanted to go to Paris with August, and follow the trail of A. But . . . Uncle Harry, my father. Would they even let us go? I tried to stamp down the doubts creeping into my head and concentrate on the adventure ahead of us.

"Miriam . . . you should come, too," August urged.

"Yes, come with us."

"Full of hope, aren't you?" She smiled. "Good. All girls your age should be. But no, I think I will stay here. My chance at love—and the book—have passed."

I wanted to argue with her, but I felt August squeeze my hand. Maybe it was better—for now— to leave it alone. But I was certain if we were able to find Etienne, I would tell him in person that Miriam still loved him. That he was her soul mate.

9

The night wind speaks her name. —A.

Miriam called the ferry service. No ferries would leave that day . . . or night. The storm raged on. I dialed Uncle Harry from my cell and told him that August and I were staying the night at Miriam's.

"How convenient," he teased. "Now listen to me, if your father had any inkling you were out there on Long Island in a beachfront house without supervision, with a sexy college student, he'd have my head. With good reason. So behave. For my sake. And yours."

I sat on a bed in one of Miriam's guest bedrooms, tracing the outline of pale blue on a quilt.

"Well, unless you want me to swim home, we're stuck here. I practically hurled my coffee on the ferry on the way over here. I just didn't think the weather was going to be this bad."

"And now you're stranded, with the smart and

devilishly handsome August, in a secluded beach house. I can just imagine what your father will say."

"Shut up," I whispered, hoping the walls weren't so thin that August could hear. "First of all, Miriam is here. It's not like there's no adult here. And my father doesn't have to know."

"Behave yourself, Calliope." I could hear his "stern" voice.

"All right, you've made your *point*," I snapped.

"I'm responsible for you this summer."

"I said . . . zip it."

"All right, but tell me what you two learned about the Book of Hours."

"Miriam thinks A. is Astrolabe."

"Heloise and Abelard's son?"

"You know who he is?"

I heard him laugh. "Yes, Callie. I'm an illuminated manuscript expert, but I was a history major in college, and . . . my master's and PhD are in medieval history. I know who Astrolabe is, even if no one knows what happened to him. He's a historical footnote. A cipher. So this A.—*our* A.—is Astrolabe?"

"Miriam thinks so." I recounted the entire story, almost word for word.

"Incredible!"

"I know."

"Wait . . . is that you sounding excited about a manuscript? One of those old goat-skin things from the freezing cold and boring auction house?"

"Yes. That's me being incredibly excited. I never knew it could be this exciting. But to know for sure, August thinks we have to take a trip."

"Someplace good?"

"Yes."

"Passports required?"

"Yes. Paris."

"The City of Light. Score one for romance! Of course, we'll have to get *that* past your dad, too."

"He just *has* to let me go. Please, Uncle Harry. Talk him into it."

"I'll try. You know how he is . . . Callie?"

"Yeah?"

"If this really is Astrolabe's book . . . it's the find of a lifetime. It's something I've been waiting for my whole life."

"I know." I smiled. The idea of Uncle Harry stumbling onto something so special made me smile. "You deserve it."

"Thanks, sweetie. You have a good night. But not *too* good. Give Miriam my best."

"She's really great, Uncle Harry. It makes me sad that she's been through so much."

"It would be nice if we could somehow get the book back to her."

"I know."

I closed my cell phone, got up from the bed, and walked downstairs to the kitchen. Miriam was preparing pasta with basil, garlic, olive oil, and tomatoes. Her hair was wet.

"I wasn't expecting that this would turn into a slumber party," she said, laughing. "I keep a kitchen garden out back. Brought in plum tomatoes and basil. Should be delicious." She chopped at a cutting board on the island in the kitchen.

"I'm so sorry about this," I said. "I feel terrible us putting you out like this."

"Nonsense. I don't get company too often."

I bit my lip.

"What?" She looked at me.

"Nothing. I . . . I guess I just wondered if you ever get visitors from your old life?"

"My daughter comes occasionally, unbeknownst to her brother and father. With her father gone, I expect that we'll see each other a little more. And I have several old, dear friends whom I go to the city to visit from time to time. We go to the Metropolitan Museum of Art. And in summer, of course, I get a few visitors for the beautiful beach. But to be honest,

I like the solitude, though I am certainly glad for your company."

"Can I help you with anything?" August asked, as he walked into the kitchen.

"No. You and Callie just go over to the table and sit. I like having people to cook for. I used to cook all the time, you know. Other wives in our social circle had personal chefs. But I liked cooking. It was the one connection Thomas and I kept. I cooked for him even when he was awful to me. It was a way, I suppose, to keep our marriage alive. To spoil him a little."

"I cook for my dad," August said.

"Professor Sokolov?" she asked.

"You know him?"

"Know of him. He's . . ." She left the comment hanging there.

"He's the one who doesn't leave the house." August smiled sadly, like he was used to people knowing that about his father.

"Yes." Miriam turned to face him. "He doesn't leave the house. But he's absolutely brilliant. I own all his books." She looked directly at August, her eyes bright, warm. I liked her even more for her kindness to August just then.

"That smells great," I said, watching as she fussed over a pan.

"And tell me," she said. She tossed garlic into the olive oil. "How long have you two been involved?"

I felt my cheeks turn bright red. "We're not really . . . involved. We just met a few days ago."

"Yes, we are," August said. "It's like fate this summer. A. brought us together."

Miriam sighed. "I remember that feeling of fate. I felt it once with Thomas. But I was wrong about him. I only experienced it one other time, with Etienne." She paused before putting the tomatoes into the sizzling oil.

"It's not too late, Miriam. Come to Paris with us," I urged.

"Yes!" August said. "Come with us."

She shook her head. "I think I'm meant to just live out my days alone. But I can be happy for you two on the hunt of this great find."

She finished cooking. I felt so horrible for her. Love wasn't supposed to be that way.

The three of us sat down to eat. Miriam lit a candle. The storm continued to howl.

Miriam asked us about school, our hobbies and interests. She asked about my parents.

"My mother died of cancer when I was a little girl. I don't really remember her." I had some memories, but they were all mixed up with Harry's stories. "I know . . . I know she and my father weren't happy with each other. And that he and Uncle Harry fought for a long time after she died. I think Harry really would have loved to raise me. Especially since my father travels a lot. And he's really not terribly cut out to be a dad. But now they have an uneasy truce. Dad works all the time, and I spend summers with Harry. One week of the summer, my grandmother on my mother's side flies in from Toronto, where she lives with her husband. I don't know him well at all; they just got married about four years ago." Really, I'd met him once or twice, and that was it. "So I still have ties to my mom, and her family. And Dad . . ." My voice trailed off. "My dad and I . . . we avoid each other. He's currently with girlfriend I've-Lost-Count and contemplating getting engaged."

"Do you think he will?" she asked gently.

"He's gotten engaged three times and never gone through with it." I laughed slightly. "The breakups are always ugly. But no, I don't know that he will get married to this one. Why ruin a perfect record? Plus it's not like he cares what I think."

"Maybe your mother was the love of his life?" Miriam suggested.

"I don't know. It doesn't sound like they had a single thing in common but me."

"Love can be a mystery," she said. "I often think of Heloise and Abelard. Their love spanned decades and morphed and changed, faced tragedy . . . and produced a child, and still endured."

"I don't know," I said. "I think people do crazy things for love." I thought about August. How from the moment I set eyes on him, I felt this crazy connection. Love made no sense.

"It does seem to render most of us temporarily insane," she said, shaking her head. "Now, listen, you two came here to find out about the book. But you must promise me that you will come back when it's sunny and beautiful, for no other reason than to go to the beach, and find sea glass, and swim."

"Promise," I said. "I love the beach but don't get to go often."

We ate our supper quietly, when the lights suddenly flickered. Then the power went out completely. We were illuminated only by the candle.

"My . . ." Miriam said. "A hazard of living on this island. I don't think they'll be on again before morning. Not with the storm." She stood and walked to the cabinets and retrieved more candles and flashlights.

She lit several more vanilla-scented candles and

placed them throughout the kitchen and the living room. After dinner, we sat and watched the night storm through the tall living room windows. The rain continued to lash, and leaves and tree branches were blown to the ground.

"It's almost like a movie," I said. "Look at it."

"I usually love the rain," Miriam said. "But this...this is a tad scary. I'm sorry you two are stuck here, but I'm grateful for the company."

I looked over at August. "Me, too."

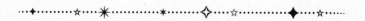

Later, Miriam lent me a pair of sweatpants and a long T-shirt for bed. She had a master bedroom on the first floor, and August and I each had a room on the second floor. My bedroom had a skylight, and I could hear the rain splattering against it. The sound was almost deafening.

A candle in a jar burned on the dresser. I sat on my bed and tried to decide if I felt sleepy. I heard a soft knock on my door.

"You up?" August whispered.

"Yeah," I called out.

He opened the door, and I stood. He was to me in three steps, then stopped, grabbed my face, stared at me in the darkness, and finally kissed me.

I honestly thought I would pass out. He didn't so much kiss me as seem to devour me, hungrily kissing me until I could barely breathe, and I was doing the same. It was like movie kissing—insane, crazed, feverish.

"I've wanted to do that since the first time we met."

"Me, too," I whispered back. We kissed in the dark, the storm making me feel like we were in our own little cocoon.

"Calliope?"

"Yeah?"

He brushed a curl from my face. "You ever think that . . . I don't know . . . your uncle's matchmaking aside, that the book wants us to be together? Even getting stranded out here. Going to Paris, maybe."

I nodded. "It's like Heloise and Abelard are reaching out to us from the book. Pushing us together. The night you texted me at three in the morning?"

"The night I couldn't sleep thinking about you . . ."

I nodded. "I had a dream. And I swear it was a

dream about Heloise and Abelard. It was a dream of being in a medieval castle or maybe even a convent. And I was searching for someone or running from something. And I'm certain you were in the dream. And the *second* I woke up, you texted me. Does that sound crazy?"

He kissed my neck, gently pressing his lips to the hollow where my collarbone was. "No," he whispered.

He kissed me again, then stopped and just touched my face. "When we go to Paris," he said, "let's go see their grave. Let's go see them."

I nodded. August pulled me closer to him. "I'm crazy about you. I can't sleep, you know. I think about you all the time."

"That's why I was awake."

I touched his stomach, which was rock hard and chiseled. Like Miriam, I felt like I understood Heloise. He was beautiful, my Abelard, my August. But it was his soul I thought I loved.

He slid a hand up my shirt. I wasn't wearing a bra, and I stiffened for a second.

"I . . ." I wanted to tell him I was a virgin. That after Charlie, I hadn't dated anyone, hadn't even *liked* anyone until him. But he stopped me.

"Don't worry. We don't have to rush. Okay? I'm not in this for some fling . . . this is real to me, Callie."

I kissed him again, and as the storm raged, I almost hoped morning would never come and we could stay there forever.

10

Treachery. What name dost thou speak?
—A.

I woke up in August's arms as a clear sky dawned pink over the Long Island Sound. I shifted slightly. We had fallen asleep in a state of undress. He had on his jeans and no shirt. I had on the sweatpants and T-shirt—no bra. I had never woken up with a guy before.

Asleep, August looked like a little boy. His hair fell across his cheeks, and his expression was utterly peaceful. His eyelids fluttered. As soon as he opened one eye, he grinned at me.

"I thought you were a dream."

I leaned down and snuggled into the crook of his arm. "Maybe I am."

I ran my fingers down his chest.

"You do that," he said breathlessly, "and we won't make the ferry."

"All right . . . I hate to leave, but we've got more plans to make."

He nodded. "Off to find Astrolabe."

After we washed up and dressed, we walked downstairs. Miriam was slicing grapefruit.

"Still no power. But the ferry's running. I called. There's one at nine twenty," she said. "Here, eat this. I can't even make coffee with no power. Not a very good hostess."

I laughed. "Well, what kind of guests arrive and unexpectedly stay the night?"

The three of us sat down at the kitchen table and ate the grapefruit.

"Will you call me as you continue searching for proof and the origins of the manuscript?"

August nodded. "We wouldn't even know the next place to look if it weren't for you."

I looked at my watch. "We better go if we're going to catch the ferry." We all stood, and I hugged Miriam. "Thank you for everything."

"Thank you," she whispered. "I hadn't been able to bear thinking about Astrolabe, but you have brought him back to life for me. Good luck."

After leaving, August and I walked to the ferry dock. A tree had been split by lightning, and puddles in the road were deep. I even saw frogs hopping about, looking rather lost.

On the ferry ride, I said, "I hate going back. It was special being there."

"I know."

Our hearts slightly heavy, we caught a cab after we arrived at Penn Station. I was dropped off at Uncle Harry's, and August headed back to his house. No one was home, so I called the auction house— Harry's direct line.

"I'm back."

"Great. Listen . . . I'm rereading the A. writings, imagining that it's Astrolabe. It certainly *sounds* like it could be him. Parents with an obsessive love affair. Tragedy. He sounds like he wants to love someone but is afraid. Afraid to end up like his father—less than a man. I mean, it really could be him, Callie." I could hear the excitement in his voice taking on a feverish quality.

"I think so, too, Harry. We have to go to Paris. We have to meet Etienne, the man who led Miriam to the book, and hear its history firsthand. Maybe we can even track down the family who owned it . . ."

"I'm working on it. We have to sort out your father and a few other things. So tell me, how are things with August?"

"Good, I mean, great, I guess. He's so amazing, I can't believe it's only been a few days we've known each other . . ."

"I knew it! Listen . . . I've got to run, sweetie. Dinner tonight?"

"Um . . . I don't know."

"Ah yes, August. Dinner tonight if you don't have dinner with August then. Or maybe the three of us can go out to eat somewhere."

"All right. I'll call you later."

"*Au revoir*. We'll get to Paris, sweetheart; see, I'm practicing my French already!"

I hung up, laughing to myself. I went into my bedroom, picked out some clothes, then took a shower. The dark circles were still there. They may have been happy dark circles, but August was definitely impinging on my beauty sleep.

I put on moisturizer, lip gloss, and added a coat of mascara to my lashes. My cell phone rang, and I answered it hurriedly when I saw it was August.

He was breathing hard. "Callie . . . ?"

"Yeah?"

"Can you come here? Please?" I heard something in his voice. Something horrible.

"What?" Panic raced through me.

"It's my dad. Come here. Please. *Please.*"

The desperation in his voice terrified me. "I'll be right there."

I ended the call, wrote a hurried note to Harry, grabbed cab money, and fled the apartment, wondering what was wrong, and praying August and the professor were okay.

When I got to Greenwich Village and August's home, he was waiting on the front steps, completely ashen.

"My God, August . . . what?" I hugged him, but he didn't hug me back. "What?" I asked more insistently.

"When I got home . . . I found him."

"What?" I wanted to shake him, wake him up from this.

"Apparently, someone broke in during the night. They ransacked the place. Definitely looking for something, Callie. And now my dad . . . he's fallen apart, Callie. This was the one place he felt safe. And now it's ruined. How can I fix it?"

I shook my head. "I don't understand—what did they want? What were they looking for?"

"The manuscript."

"Our manuscript? August . . . that's crazy. For one thing, only a handful of people know about it. For another, it's back at the auction house, under lock and key."

"Callie, you don't understand. In the insular world of antiquarians, it's known that the Rose Collection is up for sale. And I can guarantee you that people know my father was consulted. We don't know what James Rose did after we went to visit him—and if someone like the Tome Raider suspects that there's a palimpsest at stake, he could be looking for clues, same as we are."

"August, that's the second time I've heard the Tome Raider mentioned. I can't believe it's all that dangerous. He sounds more like a comic-book character than someone we should worry about."

"Then explain to me why not one single thing—like a TV or electronics, or antiques, or even the art on the walls—was taken and only our papers and books were gone through."

"I can't."

"And explain to me this: the papers are a mess, but someone treated the actual books with respect.

That sound like a common thief to you?"

"No. Are you sure nothing's taken?"

"Only one thing."

"What?"

"*Leaves of Grass*. The most valuable book we have right now."

August set his jaw. He was upset—and he was mad. He turned. "Come on."

I followed him up the steps wondering what this meant for August and his dad. And, indeed, for A.

11

Spinning lies like the spider's web. —A.

Inside, Dr. Sokolov looked broken. He sat, slumped in a dark leather chair, hair mussed, white Oxford-cloth shirt more rumpled than usual. I almost didn't recognize him. I suppose I had believed that, in that fancy brownstone, on that hushed wealthy street, in August's lush garden, in August's care for his father, that it was all just a watered-down version of helplessness and eccentricity. Not real mental illness.

But there his father sat, bereft, unable to speak clearly.

"I stayed locked in my room until August came home." He stared vacantly into space.

"Did you call nine-one-one?" I asked.

He shook his head. "August did. They should be here soon. But *Leaves of Grass*. I should have kept it in my safe." He stared up at August. "Where are my glasses?"

"On your head, Dad. Here." August tenderly

pushed the silver wire-framed glasses down until they perched on his father's nose. "Come on, let me get you upstairs until the police come."

"Can I help?" I whispered.

"Maybe boil some water for tea? Okay?"

I nodded and went to the kitchen. Hands shaking, I filled the shiny kettle with water, finding the sound of the ordinary—the faucet running, the water hitting against the inside of the kettle—somehow reassuring. I stared out at the garden.

How had the book changed everything from good to bad so quickly?

I stepped outside as the kettle nestled on the burner's flames. I walked over to the aviary and pressed up against the mesh wires. "Poor little pretty finches," I whispered. "You need your nanny birds."

The plain brown and white society finches preened a pair of electric green and blue babies, who ruffled their feathers and spread their tiny wings as if adoring their attention. A few minutes later, August stepped outside. He didn't walk over to me right away. After how close we'd become in less than a week, it hurt.

"I'm sorry, August. How could we know someone else would be on the book's trail, too?"

He shook his head. "Maybe the book is bad luck. It's cursed. It brought you to me, but look at my father . . . Someone doesn't want us finding Astrolabe."

"But we can't let that stop us." My breath left me. I needed to find Astrolabe, for Miriam. And for me. He shrugged.

I bit my lip. "August . . . it's a book. It's not the *book's* fault. And it's not your fault, either. It's not Astrolabe's fault. The book is extraordinary. You said that. Uncle Harry told me everything has its secrets, even books. I really think Astrolabe is trying to tell us something from across the centuries. He wants us to find him. To find proof of his existence. That this book was his. Until this happened, your father was as excited as any of us. He wouldn't want us to stop searching."

"Maybe," he said softly. "But look what happened when I left him alone. I can't let that happen again. How can I go to Paris?"

I could hardly face the idea of Paris, of continuing on without him. "You can't not go. This is *our* hunt. We can't let some book thief stop us."

He looked at me. "Do you understand that the palimpsest, if we can prove it belonged to Astrolabe, would be priceless? This isn't just some book, Callie. It's not a game. It's not even a detective story. If the book is what we think it is, if it truly is that valuable, there are people who would stop at nothing to get it. This whole thing could be dangerous. I don't know that we've thought this through. Not all the way."

We heard a doorbell chime.

"That'll be the police."

"Do you want me to stay?"

"You know, let me handle this. I haven't decided if we should tell them about the Book of Hours. I'll let them think this is about *Leaves of Grass.*"

"Are you sure?" If he really was right about the danger we could potentially face, I wasn't positive withholding information from the police was the smartest thing we could do.

"I'm not sure of anything right now."

I nodded, but my stomach hurt. I could see August retreating from me, the way the handwriting in the book faded when the ultraviolet light was turned off. Whereas in the bed at Miriam's we had breathed together as one, now he was pulling the air away from me. I felt like I was suffocating. My legs shook.

"Okay," I whispered.

I watched him retreat into the house. I waited in the garden for a half hour, but I felt useless. Restless. Finally, I walked to the back gate, turned the iron key, and let myself out. Even if August wasn't sure about continuing the hunt for Astrolabe, I was. Miriam's story had captivated me.

I wandered to Washington Square Park. Once there, I entered beneath the tall white stone arch and made my way to the speed chess players beneath leafy trees. I loved watching their lightning-fast moves, some concentrating intently, others using trash talk to mock their opponent.

My father played chess. He had liked me to play with him. I remember being a little girl and memorizing the shapes—the rook, the bishop, the queen, and the king. He had this enormous set, the pieces carved of marble. My little hand could scarcely wrap around the base of them. He never knew, but I used to play house with the pieces, acting out this elaborate soap opera on the chessboard. I never really enjoyed playing.

Chess, to my father, was like the law—a way to move pawns and go for the jugular on your opponent. He played ruthless chess—striking fast and without mercy—defeating me time and time again as a way to "build character" in me as a little girl. He didn't care that half the time, my eyes were brimming with tears.

I wandered the park, as in-line skaters sped past

me. I needed to talk to Harry. Instead of taking a cab, I rode the subway. I remembered August telling me he liked trains—but hated elevators. His rules made no sense to me. I worried about him, with his eccentricities like his dad. Maybe I had just been so swept up in the idea of a summer romance with a really cute guy. I started to wonder if this was just one of those relationships that starts out hot and then dies just as fast.

When I finally arrived at Harry's apartment, he wasn't home yet, and Gabe had already left for the theater. I opened the fridge and scoped the nearly barren shelves. I grabbed a Diet Coke. Shutting the fridge door, I looked at my cell phone. It had been on silent. There were four messages. All from August, but I didn't listen to them.

I shut my eyes and pictured Miriam's in the dark. August was so self-assured, and when we kissed, it had been intense. He was like no one else I'd ever met— from the instant I first saw him, I was infatuated. He wasn't like any other kind of guy. Maybe I just needed a little bit of time to chill out. After all, at the end of the summer, I'd be heading back to Boston. Maybe this whole thing was a mistake. *Calliope, be practical*, my father would say. Except, for a mistake, it felt so perfect.

At loose ends, I wandered into Harry's small office area and started pulling the "Mom books" down from his bookshelf. He had photo albums from their childhood, and then from when they both moved to New York City together after college. They're hilarious. Can I just say big shoulder pads in the '80s were a huge fashion tragedy? I'm not sure what my mom was thinking—and Harry was worse. There are even a few pictures of him in some kind of refugee-from-a-New-Wave-band getup. Positively horrifying!

It was comforting to me to go through the books. One after the other, I turned pages. There were pictures of my parents' wedding. My mother wore a sliplike dress of long ivory satin and carried a simple bouquet of daisies, with a couple of flowers in her hair, no veil. She and my father looked happy—in fact, it was an uncharacteristic picture of him, since he usually favored what I called "the Scowl."

There were pictures of me when I was first born. Then there was a lengthy gap in pictures, which was where I usually stopped looking at pictures. But for some reason, today I pressed on to just a few pages of photos of her with no hair, wearing a scarf, deep circles under her eyes. Harry was in a few of them, lying next to her in her bed, the two of them smiling for the camera. In two, there was a man I didn't recognize. I made a mental note to ask Harry who he was.

Bored, I opened the doors to cabinets beneath the bookshelf. I wasn't intending to snoop or anything, I was just looking for more Mom boxes. There was a box with my name on it. It wasn't a present, but a box filled with more old stuff of my mom's. I could tell, since a high school yearbook peeked over the top of it.

I pulled it out, excited. Harry had never shown me this before, and I wondered why. Her old yearbooks were haphazardly stored with a trophy from a singing competition and several cards from old boyfriends. They were the things of a girl's teenage years, the treasures of her life. I had things just like them in my room at home.

Except for one envelope. I picked it up, an expensive, heavy-linen envelope that had the name of a law firm in Boston in the upper-left corner. I opened it.

They were divorce papers. From my father. Against my mother.

My heart slammed against my rib cage. I had told myself that, different though they were, they had some kind of amazing love story, a love story

I would understand when I got older. But here were papers that proved otherwise.

I looked at the date through blurry tears of disbelief. He had sued her for divorce as she was *dying*.

I shoved the papers back in the envelope, pushed the envelope into the box, put the box back in the cabinet, and slammed the cabinet doors shut. Now I had even more reason to hate my dad. How could he do that to her? She had been diagnosed with cancer. What kind of man abandons a woman when she is sick?

I waited for Harry. When the apartment door opened, he smiled at me. "Hey… are you and August coming to dinner with me?"

I shook my head. "Not tonight." I wiped at tears that had pushed their way to the brims of my eyes.

"What's wrong?"

First I told him about the break-in.

"I'll call the Sokolovs right away. He has an alarm system, but my guess is he didn't have it on. And until we know for sure why someone broke in, August and his dad should be careful. And so should you, for that matter. I should let security at the auction house know, just in case." He reached for his cell. "Callie, maybe I was wrong to send you on this chase with August. You're just kids, and there's real danger here. The stakes are higher than I thought."

"No. I'm not stopping."

"Callie—"

I shook my head and held up my hand. "I can't explain it, Harry, but I have to prove the book belonged to Astrolabe."

Harry smiled. "Ah. You've been bitten by the history bug."

"Maybe."

"Fine. But from now on, you can stick to *books* and research. I can only *imagine* what your father would do to me if you came face-to-face with a major thief like the Tome Raider or something worse."

"Yeah, Dad. That's the other reason I'm upset."

"What about him?"

"I found something today. A box . . . " I let my voice trail off, and Harry's eyes darted to the cabinet.

"The box with my name on it, Harry. I found the divorce papers."

Harry sat down in the plush chair opposite me. "You're going to have to ask your father, Callie."

"That's bull, Harry. No. *You're* the one I'm close to. You tell me."

"I can't."

"You mean you won't."

"No, I can't. Do you even realize the negotiations I had to go through with your father to get this summer thing worked out? To just be able to see you? It would kill me to lose contact with you, Callie."

"I'm sixteen. What is he going to do? Take away my cell phone? My computer? Not let me talk to you? And what about when he travels? I mean, come on, Harry."

"I don't want to cross him. You have no idea how he can be."

"Hello? I'm his *daughter,* remember? I totally know what he can be like."

"Callie, I have to keep the peace with him. Grandma's coming to see you this summer . . . We've already lost so much. So for the sake of your grandmother and Gabe and me, there are some things I avoid talking about."

"So you've been lying to me all these years?"

"No, not lying, exactly."

"What then, *exactly*?"

"I just promised your father I wouldn't talk about it."

"Well, you're going to have to now. Come on,

Harry. What happened? How could he divorce her when she was sick, when she was dying in the hospital? Who does that!? And for that matter, I saw those pictures from then, after she had lost her hair. Why isn't Dad there? Who's that guy in the hospital room with all of you?"

Harry stared at me, saying nothing. But I didn't back down. "You loved my mother, Harry. She was your sister and your best friend. You owe it to her. To me. I *deserve* to know about her life. I am tired of her being as . . . as much of a mystery to me as A. She was *my mother*."

All my life, my curiosity about my mother was always squashed. I'd ask questions, and Harry or my grandmother or my father would carefully dart around them. Harry would show me beautiful pictures of her and tell me pretty, happy, shiny stories as bright as Christmas presents. They were stories that reminded me of fairy tales, of princesses and ribbons and bright stars. And my father told me nothing. Neither good, nor bad. It was as if she had never existed.

Harry was quiet for a long while. "You're right. You do deserve to know."

I tapped the arm of the love seat.

"She . . . Your mother and your father never had

what I would call a healthy relationship." He exhaled. "Who am I kidding? They were relationship *napalm*."

I could believe it. Somehow, it felt as if I were finally hearing the *truth*.

"Napalm. They were horrible for each other. But he fell madly in love with her. And to be honest, it hasn't been like that with any of the women since. Sure, I've seen girlfriends come and go with your dad. But this was different. Your mother was so beautiful, and she really didn't want to get married. She was a free spirit, and he's . . . your father. I think he figured that he could tame her. That he could turn her into this perfect little lawyer's wife, a beautiful bird in a gilded cage."

"That's exactly like Miriam Rose."

"A bit. He swept her off her feet, you know. The full-court press. Rooms full of flowers. He once found out she liked lilies of the valley, and at the time, they could only be found—that season—in Hawaii. He special-ordered huge bouquets of them. It must have cost him a fortune. Candlelight dinners at Manhattan's hottest restaurants, Broadway shows, yacht cruises. I guess after a while, she thought that he really loved her and that they could make it work."

"And?" I held my breath.

"Marriage doesn't *change* a person, Calliope. She was still the same free spirit. You could dress her up in a black Chanel dress . . . but she was your mother. She loved to go out dancing and she loved her artsy friends in Soho, and she hung with a bunch of crazy modern-art painters in Brooklyn who'd been squatting in an old building there, this loft where they made films and painted and . . . it was just a wild scene. Trust me, there are films of your mom painting naked somewhere." He laughed. "She was unstoppable. This ball of energy and ideas. Singing with a band."

"Okay," I said. "That doesn't sound like anything my dad would be involved with. Not at *all*."

"Exactly. It was like everyone could see it—but them."

"Didn't you try to talk some sense into her?"

"I loved my sister, but no one could tell her anything. Just like no one can tell your father anything. They were totally alike in that way. Anyway, within . . . I don't know, six months of the wedding, they were at each other's throats. You know how your dad is. He came down hard on her. Always criticizing. She wanted to leave him, but she showed up on my doorstep pregnant. She felt trapped."

"She could have just had me . . . and left him. Raised me as a single mother."

"I think part of her loved him. She gave him one more chance. But the pregnancy didn't help. They fought horribly. One time, they were screaming so loudly a neighbor called the police. Maybe someone else might have handled it differently, but your mom started getting very nervous, anxious, depressed. Your father accused her of being a bad mother."

I felt as if the world stopped. I heard Harry. I heard him say the words from somewhere far away, like hearing a voice above the storm at Miriam's. "But she was a good mother. I remember her. I remember us painting together. Finger painting."

"Yes. *On the walls*. Stuff like that drove your father—in a word—*insane*. I thought . . . I really thought she was going to have a nervous breakdown. I considered getting her to agree to go to a hospital. Then she started acting all happy again. Out of the blue."

"What was it? Did they finally work out their differences?"

"No. She had fallen in love again. She was having an affair."

"What?" *How did I know none of this?*

"Don't judge her for it, Callie."

"So was he . . . he the guy in the picture? Next to her in the hospital bed?"

Uncle Harry nodded. "The man in the picture made her happy. He saved her, in a lot of ways, before she got sick. He calmed her down, made her joyful again. Then she found out she had ovarian cancer. And that was . . . it. Stage four. He was with her. She chose him over your dad to go to treatment with. She lived a separate life from your dad. And you. She lived in an apartment near the hospital. It made treatment easier."

"But . . . I don't understand. He never said anything about a separation."

"It wasn't a true legal separation. She couldn't be around you during treatment. Her immune system . . . Kids are like miniature germ factories. And, well, she didn't want you to see her like that. She'd see you on visits, but she was fighting for her life. And I guess I really thought that after all your father had put her through, he would just let her die in peace. But he didn't. He served her divorce papers in the hospital . . . fought her to her dying breath."

"So who is the man? The one she fell in love with. What's his name?"

"Raphael."

My knees shook. "I used to ask about a Raphael. When I was little. My father told me Raphael was an angel. That I must have heard the story in Sunday school. And to forget about it."

"He was a good man. He lives here in the city. Married and then divorced. No kids. I see him maybe once a year for lunch. He's a photographer. Has had showings in a couple of galleries. He asks after you every time. I don't think he ever got over your mother completely."

"Uncle Harry . . . I don't understand. Why would my father be so heartless? Why would he try to destroy her when she was already dying?"

"He loved her. And it's the way your father loves. He . . . he consumes people. Your mother loved you very much. She just . . . she and your father were two people who tried their damndest to destroy each other. And in some ways, they both succeeded."

"This is too much, Harry. I— I need to be alone for a little bit." I jumped from the chair, my heart slamming against my chest, and went into my bedroom.

And there, alone, I cried. At first, it was a weird aimless crying. I cried for Miriam, for August, for

Professor Sokolov, for Astrolabe and Heloise and Abelard. And then, finally, I felt the hard tears start, and I cried for me. For the motherless little girl and the woman in the picture in my room whom I never had the chance to know.

12

How much has my mother lost because of her beloved? —A.

Harry rapped gently on my door. "Come out, Calliope. You need to eat something."

"Please go away, Harry." I sniffled. I rolled onto my side and pulled the pillow into my stomach.

"None of this changes how much she loved you, Calliope. She doted on you. It doesn't change how much Gabe and I love you."

"I said go away. Please, Harry. Just go away."

"All right." His voice sounded choked. "If you want to talk, come to my room. It's not like I'll be able to sleep anyway."

I listened as his footsteps grew quieter as he walked down the hall. Aggie was sleeping on my pillow, and I lay down next to him and listened to him purr, sliding my fingers through his velvety fur, almost absentmindedly.

"Oh, Aggie," I whispered, wiping at my eyes.

"How can things turn from so wonderful, so happy, so perfect, to ruined? How?"

I turned my head. I had a picture of my mother in a small silver frame on my desk. I looked at it. I really never knew her. I had a few memories. But they were just quick flashes, not a fluid continuous narrative of our life together. I remembered a song she used to sing, this humming song, actually, with no words.

Sometimes, I thought I remembered a smell. Lilies of the valley reminded me of her. I remembered finger painting. And making cookies one time. And then there was the one dark memory, her crying. I remember tugging at her shirt, trying to get her to stop crying, and she crumbled to the floor. I remember touching her hair, "making nice" I used to call it. But I don't remember anything else. Not really.

Sometimes, I looked at pictures of her, and I would *think* I remembered. But I knew in my heart it was more like filling in the gaps—seeing the pictures and making up a memory. Or I filled in Harry's pretty stories, tied up with ribbon, and made them a little present I called my own. But they were gifts from Harry and not really mine.

At some point, I dozed off. When I woke, I could hear Harry yelling. He never yelled. Except at my father. I guessed that was who was on the other end of the phone. I sat up and crept to the door, but I couldn't make out any words, just the tone.

I changed into my pajamas. My stomach growled, but I didn't want to see Harry. I heard his footsteps in the hall again.

"Callie, hon . . . August has called your cell phone fifty times, I think. It's on silent, on the coffee table, but I can see it lighting up. Don't you want to talk to him?"

"No."

"How about something to eat? I'll make you some soup. Or I'll go down to the store and get you Chunky Monkey ice cream, or whatever you want."

I didn't answer.

"Can I come in?"

I sighed and unlocked the door, but I didn't turn the knob. He opened the door and poked his head in.

"I should have told you." He stepped all the way in and sat on my bed. "But you know, the only two people who know what goes on in a relationship are the two people in it. It wasn't my place to tell you. And I thought, eventually, if you wanted to learn more when you were older, that was when I would explain what I knew. I didn't know if you would be angry at Raphael. At your mother. At your father. Raphael has some beautiful portraits of her, and it has always been his intention to give you one someday. But . . . when you asked questions, I sort of told you the fairy tales I thought you wanted to hear."

"But I really just wanted to *know* her. That's one reason I love spending time with you. You're my connection to who she was."

"In my defense? Your spending time with Gabe and me? It's not like any formal arrangement. With your dad, I always feel like I'm at the whim of the emperor. I didn't want to risk his cutting me off from you. I *couldn't* risk that. After your mother died, he excised her family from your life. Your grandma had already lost her daughter. She didn't need to lose her granddaughter, too." He paused, then continued. "So we just agreed to avoid the difficult topics. We agreed—your grandmother, Gabe, and I, among ourselves—that we would do whatever it took to keep you in our lives. So if you asked about your mom, we just stuck to the good stuff."

"He can't control me anymore, Uncle Harry. I can make up my own mind who I want to see, where I want to live even."

He shrugged. "I know. Now I know." He looked over at the bookshelf at the picture he kept of my mother, the one of her laughing. "She was so special. She was. You remind me of her, sometimes. How you hope for things. You're not the typical jaded teenager. She believed in love. She believed in wishing on a star. Finding lucky pennies. She would go whole blocks not stepping on the crack." He laughed. "She was winsome. She would believe in Astrolabe. She would be here with us—I know it. Hunting for the history of the book. That would be like her. The only thing she believed in that she shouldn't have? That she could make things work with your dad. That two people so fundamentally toxic together could figure out a way to live happily ever after."

"You told Dad I know about the divorce papers? The affair? I heard you shouting."

He nodded. "He'll be here Friday. Staying until Sunday, then off to the L.A. office. Negotiating some entertainment deal out there for that record label."

"I don't want to see him."

"I don't know that you have a choice."

"I hate him right now."

Uncle Harry exhaled slowly. "I've never been a big fan of his. And I kind of hate him, too, sometimes. But he's your dad, which means I'm stuck with him and have to get along with him. And you are most certainly stuck with him."

"Was he ever nice?"

"Yeah. When he was trying to win over your mother. . . . He was a pretty romantic guy."

I sighed. "I guess I don't really have a choice. I have to see him. I have to talk to him."

"And what about August?"

"I'll call him back."

He handed me my cell phone. "I'd say he's crazy about you."

"What if I end up like my mother? What if love ruins everything? What if we're really not good for each other?"

"There are people like your mom and dad . . . and then there are people like Gabe and me. People who somehow make it work. You'll figure it out, sweetie."

"Thanks."

He hugged me. "Calliope . . . I love you like you're my own daughter. So does Gabe. Know that, okay? I would never hurt you intentionally. I promise, from now on, if you ask me a question, you'll get the truth. The real truth."

"I know." I wrapped my arms around his neck and felt tears spilling again. "I really love you. Thanks, Harry."

"Call August."

"I will."

After Uncle Harry left my room, I shut the door again and dialed August.

"Where were you?" he asked. He didn't even say hello. "I came into the garden and you were gone."

"I needed to think. And then when I got back here, I needed to talk to Harry. About my mother."

"Are you okay?"

"Sort of. I'll tell you about it when I see you next. It's kind of ... huge. What about you? Are you okay? What about your dad?"

"You know, he's calmer now ... but he's worried about us, about the trail of the book."

"I'm not stopping." I said firmly. "I don't care who's worried. I'm not."

"Really?"

I felt a flash of anger. "No. I already told Harry. I won't stop. Not for you. Not for anyone."

There was a long silence. I was almost afraid of what his response would be. Then one word. "Good."

"Really?"

"I'm going to Paris. I haven't told my dad yet, but a piece of me is really pissed that someone broke into my house and stole *Leaves of Grass*. They are not going to chase me off the Book of Hours."

"Then I'm going, too."

"Harry called my dad. He said you weren't . . . you couldn't."

"Well, I am. I'm going. I don't care if I have to sneak on the plane."

"Really?"

"Really. I know it sounds crazy, but . . . after talking to Harry about my mother, I have to. I can't explain it, but I'm following the story of Heloise and Abelard all the way to the end."

"I was hoping you'd say that. But for now, let's keep this between us. Because we may just have to go to Paris on our own."

I swallowed. My dad would so kill me. And for the first time, so would Harry. But I was going to do it.

"I need to find out the truth about the book. Astrolabe had something to say. He deserves for people to know he existed."

"My dad is coming," he whispered. "I'll call you later."

I ended the call. In my mind, I saw three women: Heloise, Miriam, and my mother. All nearly silenced.

I wasn't going to let that happen. I was going to

find out what was really said in the Book of Hours, in the palimpsest. In the whispered writings beneath the illuminated paintings. In the words of A., who knew what it was like to be the child of parents whose love nearly destroyed each other.

A. was me. Maybe not me, exactly, but a lot like me.

And I would go to Paris to learn more.

Even if it meant getting into a whole lot of trouble.

13

My father . . . destroyer, creator. —A.

"Calliope, you haven't touched your lobster." My father sat across from me, sipping his favorite 2001 Bordeaux wine.

"I'm not hungry." I moved my fork around the plump lobster flesh, dripping in butter, and bit my lip.

"You sound like a petulant child."

"And you sound like an overbearing father."

A violinist in a long black gown played at the far end of the dining room. Periodically, our waiter hovered, clearing away plates, bringing fresh bread, and otherwise fussing unobtrusively. The restaurant was one of my father's favorites, a place where he could easily spend five hundred dollars on dinner for the two of us. He always said he was paying for the view, which stretched out from the window by our table, affording us the sight of all of Central Park.

"Calliope . . ." Dad sighed in his usual impatient way.

"You should have told me. About my mother. About what you did to her when she was sick."

I saw the anger flash in his eyes, even after all that time. Like Harry said. *Napalm.* "What about what she did to *me*?"

"It's been how many years? I still deserved to know the whole story."

"You were too young." He said it in this offhand way, as if he was telling me that I was too young to learn where babies came from, or that Santa Claus was a lie.

"I'm not too young now. You *lied* to me. You told me nothing about her. Not the real story of the two of you. She's my *mother*."

"The sin of omission is not the same as a lie."

"Right," I snapped. "The way you don't want to know if a client is doing something illegal, right? That way you can pretend what you do isn't immoral."

"I'm a lawyer. *I'm* not a criminal. And when *you're* a lawyer, someday, you'll understand."

"No, I won't."

"Of course you will."

"No, I won't." I took a sip of my water. "Because I'm never going to *be* a lawyer."

"That's ridiculous. You have a perfect GPA.

You've been planning on pre-law since middle school. Harvard. That's been your plan."

"No, Dad, that's been *your* plan."

"Calliope." He set down his linen napkin. "Just because you're upset with me is no reason to derail your entire life."

"I'm going to major in history." I blurted it out. Even *my* eyes widened. I hadn't known I was going to say that. I hadn't even really thought it. But now that I said it, it felt so right.

"What the hell," he hissed, "are you going to do with a degree in history? It's useless. What? Be a teacher?"

"Maybe I'll be like Uncle Harry."

I could see the heat rising off of him. "No. And another thing, young lady, two months before the start of your senior year is no time to be getting involved in a serious relationship. So whoever this boy is who Harry mentioned, I say move on. Forget him and concentrate on your studies."

I looked across the table at him. When I was very young, I had nannies, and then when I got older, Uncle Harry stepped in when my father traveled in summer, which was constantly. The neighbor across the hall. Sofia's family. Even occasional girlfriends of my dad would watch over me, foolishly believing that if we bonded, my dad would finally propose. Or they'd get a proposal and then hope he'd actually go through with a wedding.

Like a Gouldian finch, I'd been raised by everyone but my dad. Dinners together were rare. It seemed like the only way he kept tabs on me at all was my report card. Somehow, bringing home straight As every semester was his sign that I was perfect, that my life plan, my world, was unfolding just as he wanted.

But he was a stranger.

I was tired of hating him. "You know, Dad . . . you don't even know me."

"Don't even know my own daughter? I think that's a bit ridiculous, don't you? A bit over the top, *even for you*."

We looked alike. Something about our noses was similar. The way, when I turned, my profile was like his. His hair was graying at the temples, but was still thick. He weighed the same—as he was happy to tell anyone who would listen—as when he'd rowed crew at Harvard. He could still run five miles on the treadmill without losing his breath. Everywhere we went, women looked at him. He reminded me of a soap opera actor—all perfect teeth and perfect hair and perfect suits. But hollow, as if it was all a scripted, vapid performance.

"No, Dad. I'm not being ridiculous. You don't know *me*. You know my *achievements*."

"We are what we achieve."

I rolled my eyes. "What? Is that Lawyer Zen?"

He smiled at me. "You were always very quick-witted, Calliope. I know that about you. I"—I saw him struggle to say it—"like that about you."

"If you know me so well, what's my favorite color?"

"Pink."

"Why? Because I painted my room that color in third grade? It hasn't been my favorite color since I was nine. Then I went through a purple phase. But no, since junior high it's been green."

"Just because—"

"I'm not done. What's my favorite movie?"

"You like lots of movies."

"There's *one* favorite, though, Dad."

"I have no idea. *The Godfather?*"

I rolled my eyes. "No. That's *your* favorite movie. Though you like *Godfather II* almost as much. My favorite movie is *Breakfast at Tiffany's.*"

"Really?"

"Yes, really. And what's my favorite place in the whole world?"

"You love Hawaii."

"Nope."

"Well, then Manhattan. You've always loved coming here with your mother's brother."

"Be more specific."

"Where then?"

I could see him clench his jaw a little. He didn't like not knowing the answer to everything.

"I think it's August's garden. Down in Greenwich Village. It's the most peaceful place I've ever been to."

"That boy."

"Yes, Dad. That boy."

"It's a mistake, Calliope. Love at your age can only distract you from school, from college, from accomplishing all your goals."

"What if instead it made me happy?"

My father narrowed his eyes. "What?"

"You know . . . this crazy thing called emotions? Happiness. You've heard of it, haven't you?"

"There's no need to be rude, Calliope."

"I'm not her."

"What do you mean?"

"Are you afraid I'll take after her? Is that why

you don't want me to have a boyfriend? To have a life? Because you made her so unhappy, so utterly miserable? Is that it? You have to make sure everyone around you is unhappy. I'm not like her."

"I know you're not her. Your mother was . . ."

"What?"

"Never mind."

"No. *What*? That's the thing, Dad. You never tell me who she was. Did you even know? I mean, the way Harry tells it, you were nothing alike. So why did you even marry her?"

My father sipped his wine. A *big* sip. I watched him blink a couple of times. Like he was gathering his thoughts. My father *never* gathers his thoughts. He launches into two-hour closing arguments without notes.

"To be honest? It's funny that you say your favorite movie is *Breakfast at Tiffany's*. Because she was my Holly Golightly."

"Mom wasn't interested in being a socialite. In money."

"No. But she was madcap and eccentric, and she was gorgeous. I saw her . . . and I guess, I didn't stop to think. All my life, I've made the hard decisions. I really have. I've set aside what I *wanted* for what was the right thing to do."

"What do you mean?" I played with my lobster, looking at my father just partway. I didn't know what I wanted to hear.

"When I was a boy, I followed my father's footsteps. Into the law. My younger brother, your uncle Anthony, he got off easy."

"What do you mean?" I'd met my uncle Tony only three times, and even then, it had been years.

"He was a screwup. They expected nothing from him. And he was only too happy to oblige. But me? My father's hopes were pinned on me."

"Couldn't you have told him? Told your parents that you might want to do something else?"

He shook his head. "We're talking about a legal and financial *dynasty*. My father intended to hand over the law firm to me. Anthony got a free pass to join a fraternity, spend his trust fund, and be a drunkard."

"Well, what would you have studied if you hadn't become a lawyer?"

"I don't know. It was so long ago, Calliope. I guess I don't remember a time when the expectation wasn't there. I know, for a while, I daydreamed of owning a restaurant. But now I just eat in the best of the best and collect wine. So in a way, I suppose it all worked out."

"Do you hate your brother because he got to do what he wanted? And you had to follow the rules?"

"No. It's not like that. But after law school, after your grandfather died, you know, I just kept doing the right thing. And then the next right thing. I put in, on a good day, fourteen hours at the office. I was on a plane fifteen or twenty days out of every month—New York, L.A., Miami. I lived with a bottle of Mylanta in my briefcase. And then, I will never forget . . . I got invited to the unveiling of a new exhibit at the Whitney. Not the Metropolitan Museum of Art, where it would be the same crowd of snobs. But an avant-garde exhibit. It was backed by a rather insane client of mine, a German industrialist who just loved to fund these crazy, expensive installations. He invited me. I showed up. To this day, I don't know why."

"Fate." By now I had dropped all pretense of playing with my food. This was the most my father had ever talked to me at one time in my entire life.

"I don't believe in fate, Calliope. But if you want to call it that, then fine. I walked in. And there she was."

"At the party?"

He laughed. "No. *In* the exhibit."

I laughed. "What? What are you talking about?"

He nodded. "In the exhibit. She was *in* the exhibit. It was about the soullessness of the modern world, and she was supposed to be this wraith, this ghost, inside of a computer or a machine. I can't even tell you what the hell the damn thing was supposed to mean." He started laughing. Not a quiet laugh, but this laugh that came from a place I didn't think my dad went to that often. He looked lighter than he had in a long time.

"Okaaaaaaaaaaaaaay," I said, drawing the word out. "So you met my mother while she was pretending to be inside a computer in a museum exhibit."

"Exactly. But it was this amazing opportunity. You see, everyone was *supposed* to be staring at her. So I could look and look, and it was completely . . . what was supposed to be happening. I could stare all I wanted. And then, at this one moment, even though she was supposed to be this wraith, this dead woman or whatever the heck she was, she suddenly dropped her act. She dropped the persona . . . and looked at me. Right at me. And at that moment, I decided I had to meet her, had to have her."

"Does Harry know how you met?"

Dad shook his head. "I don't know. Maybe. I didn't think anyone did. I couldn't really imagine how I would explain to my family that the woman I was crazy about was this wild child, free spirit from inside a piece of art."

"So how did my mother fall in love with you? You weren't her type, right?"

"Not at all. At first we sort of amused each other, I think. She was spontaneous. She'd call me at the office and demand that I take a dinner break—which would turn out to be hot dogs at a Yankees game. She would wake up on a Sunday and decide we should rent a car and drive to Maryland to eat soft-shell crab. She would walk ten blocks without stepping on a crack because it would break her mother's back . . . She collected found pennies and kept them in a lucky jar. For my part, I think she really did enjoy shaking me out of my routine, but it was a kick to her getting front-row theater tickets and going to different restaurants, and traveling to Paris, and...."

"Paris?"

He nodded. "Yes. I proposed to her in Paris."

I shut my mouth. But . . . I had to ask.

"Did you ever go to see the grave of Heloise and Abelard?"

My father looked at me as if it was a revelation. "That is the oddest question, Calliope, but we did.

The lovers. There's apparently a myth associated with leaving a letter on their grave. I don't remember it. It was something your mother was into. She was very superstitious. She liked getting her palm read. *She* believed in fate."

"So how did it go all wrong?" *Did anyone make it work? Really? Could you start from napalm and fire and attraction and not ruin it somehow?*

"Mostly it was my fault. I think I confused love with ownership. And when she . . . truly rejected me, I . . ." He looked away. "I know you're very angry right now, but I want you to know that before she died, I visited her in her hospital room. We forgave each other, you know. That's why the papers are unsigned. I wish I could undo those last months."

"Did she know she was going to die?"

He nodded. "Right after we got married, it was obvious that your mother and I had made a huge mistake. Opposites attract, but in our case, we were so unhealthy for each other. I wanted her to change. I wanted her to understand that the reason I was never home was for her—that I was building something for *us*. And she was sure that if I loved her enough, I would change. I hurt her. She hurt me. And I guess I didn't see how desperate she was for me to understand her." He looked so sad, but continued on. "You're right. I make the people around me unhappy. It's how I am. It's what I do. And at the end when she needed me to stop fighting her, I . . . couldn't."

I suddenly felt this crushing guilt settling like a rock in my rib cage.

"I didn't mean that when I said you make the people around you unhappy."

"Yes, you did. And you're not totally wrong. After your mother died, I just stopped being the human being I could have been if she were alive."

I blinked back tears. "Even if you two were a disaster, I wish . . . I wish I had her here."

His chin trembled slightly. "Some people are like shooting stars. They burst through our lives in a spectacular arc, but they don't stay long. They just leave a trail."

14

I knew her as I knew my own face. —A.

On Sunday, my father and I had brunch together. Dad had asked me to bring August, but I didn't think we had made *that* much progress. Baby steps. When I said good-bye to Dad, I hugged him a little harder. "Have a good trip."

"Are you going back to Harry's or over to that boy's house?"

"You mean August? You can say his name, Dad. We have plans, and I'm going to Harry's later."

He picked up his suitcase in the lobby of his hotel and turned to go. Then he stopped, his back still to me. "I promise to try a little harder, Calliope. Maybe we can each try."

I watched him walk away from me. We had a long way to go, but maybe now with truth, we would have a chance.

August and I were meeting at his house. My father had made his stance on a trip to Paris crystal clear.

I had tried reasoning (well, begging would be more like it) with Uncle Harry about going to Paris, but he insisted that the museum would use contacts in Europe to follow the trail. The break-in, in his opinion, made it too dangerous for us to continue in our quest for information about the palimpsest. Notes that Dr. Sokolov had scribbled about it had vanished along with *Leaves of Grass*. And though he was an absentminded professor, both he and August insisted the palimpsest was far too important for him to have misplaced his notes.

According to Harry, given the circumstances, August and I were officially "off the case."

But August and I had other ideas.

I took the subway, the subterranean station hot and causing my hair to curl into even tighter ringlets. When the car whooshed into the station, I stepped on, grateful for the blast of air-conditioning. I found a seat easily—it was nearly empty on a Sunday afternoon—and rode it to Greenwich Village. I walked hurriedly to August's house and decided not to ring the bell. Instead, I walked around the block and found the wrought-iron gate, covered with a trellis of ivy, leading to his garden. Cautiously, I opened the gate. I saw him, feeding the finches, whispering to them. I felt like my insides dropped to the ground, this rush of wanting his arms around me, of wanting everything to be okay.

I think he felt me staring at him, because he turned and looked right at me. He dropped the dish he was cleaning and came to me. I don't remember running to him, but I know we were together in an instant, my arms around his neck, his mouth on mine.

We kissed so hard, we literally sank to our knees. I couldn't breathe. I couldn't think. I just wanted to kiss him harder. I hadn't seen him in days, and I surprised myself with the intensity of feeling I had for him. How much I'd missed him in that short time.

"I'm sorry about everything," he said finally, pulling his mouth from mine and instead pressing it against my ear. "I was worried if you saw your dad that he would somehow talk you out of our being together."

"No. My father couldn't talk me out of anything. He tried, for about half a minute," I said.

"I was worried that you would doubt us—that either my behavior or something he said would make you not believe in us. Make you think that crazy-love always turns spiteful and hateful. That people can't be together without ruining it."

"I thought that, too. For a second. Though our going to Paris will..." I had a moment of regret. "It'll definitely make my dad and Harry really angry."

"We don't have to go, Calliope. We don't. Deep down, I feel positive it's Astrolabe's book. That's enough for me."

"I can't explain it, but I have to know more about the book. I have to know in my heart that Astrolabe existed and wrote it, and that he somehow survived his parents' tragedy. That I'll survive my parents' insanity. That you will survive your mother's leaving and your father's phobias."

"Callie." He kissed my neck, and I felt his hands slide slightly into the waistband of my jeans. "I know it's crazy, but I'm falling for you."

"Me, too."

Saying it made sense to me. I wanted to say it. I wanted it to be real.

He pushed my curls back from my face. "I've got leads in Paris. This is your last chance. I can go alone and you won't have to upset Harry. Or maybe you can talk him into it."

"No. His mind is made up, and so is mine. I'm going. This has been *ours* from the start."

"Are you sure?"

"Positive."

"That settles it then."

"Who's going to watch your dad while you're gone? And the birds and the garden?"

"Well . . . the last two days I've been doing a lot of thinking. I need to let go a little bit. My father's got a graduate student. His name's Khalil. He said he would check on my father every day. Handle the things I do. I'm going with you, Calliope. We're going to their tomb."

"Okay," I said. And even though it was really hot in the garden, I shivered slightly.

Paris.

The secrets of the book.

I didn't get home to Harry's until almost eleven. He was sitting with Gabe, drinking red wine.

"If it isn't our wayward niece," Harry said. "Where have you been? As if I have to ask."

"I went to see August."

Harry grinned. "My matchmaking skills remain

unsurpassed. I'm assuming your father made it off all right. Otherwise, I know we would have heard. And you'll be happy to know, on the good-news front, I left you some books on your bed."

"What about?"

"What do you think? Them. Heloise, Abelard. You may not be going to Paris, but you can read about her. Their letters. You know she was quite racy for her time."

"Really?"

I sat next to the two of them. I always marveled at how every line on Uncle Harry's face relaxed when he was around Gabe. They never argued. They still, years later, did little things for each other. Gabe prepared lunch for Harry every day and walked over to the auction house. They ate together and then took a stroll. Harry always laid out Gabe's orange juice and this pill he took for his cholesterol every day, just so, on the counter. They still left each other these ridiculous love notes on Post-its on the bathroom mirror.

"Yes," Harry said. "She and Abelard were . . . how shall I put this . . . absolutely naughty in the rectory of a convent."

"You're kidding me!"

"No. Everyone thinks this generation is so sex-crazed. Well, they were wild a thousand years ago—absolutely crazy in love. Anyway, I thought you might want to read some more about them."

"Thanks."

"I'm sorry about Paris, but we'll get there eventually."

The guilt pinged at my heart, but I leaned down to kiss each of them and then went to my room to read about Heloise. Before she entered the convent, her religion was love. She lived and breathed for Abelard, and thought of him even when she was supposed to be praying.

I read their letters—over and over again. Eight of them originally survived, and then a secret cache of letters was found years later. Their passion was woven on the pages, each writing of a love that burned bright. She wrote of Abelard as a blood-red rose. She was his precious jewel.

She said men thought her chaste, but secretly she wanted and longed for her tutor, Abelard, who moved into her home, where they shared their passion while hiding it from her uncle. When Abelard became a hermit, she was relentless in trying to lure him back into society—and back into her life.

Twelve years later, they resumed correspondence. By then, she probed his mind about religious and doctrinal questions, chastising him occasionally for his morose nature. I thought about how serious August was, how super-responsible. Maybe he was a bit like Abelard.

But it also sounded like Abelard went a little crazy. He was paranoid—he had become hated by some of the monks in his order, and he thought they were trying to poison him. Heloise sought his friendship; he sought her wise counsel. The passion had cooled.

Cooled, but I was certain an ember remained. He made it clear—agonizingly clear—all those years later, that he wanted to be buried beside her. To rest forever next to her, side by side, in a way they hadn't been able to in life.

I wondered about them, the jewel and the rose. I couldn't imagine any love surviving a lack of communication for twelve years. I couldn't imagine, now that I was so certain of how I felt about August, going a *day* without seeing him, let alone years. Every time I thought of going back to Boston, it seemed dark and dreary. So how could Heloise be so certain of how she felt? My cell phone rang.

"You there?" August asked when I connected.

"Yeah."

"I wish you were still here. I miss you."

"Me, too. I've been reading about Heloise. Do you know they were wild before their time?"

He laughed. "Yeah. I've been Googling them and checking out their story. And my dad has a few books."

"What about Astrolabe? Can you imagine being their child? Of this love story that was so powerful, that they were famous—*literally* famous—in their time. And everyone would know. You'd carry this burden of being the child of this tragic love affair. And now your mother's a nun, and your father's a hermit. Heck, it makes my parents' love story sound like a bed of roses. And Astrolabe would grow up knowing that once—for this period of time—they loved each other so much that it was obsession. And what they lost. I mean, if I were him, I would never want to love anyone. It would scare me too much."

"Or you might be the opposite."

"How?"

"You'd want to find a love that rivaled that. How many people get to find that kind of love? That insane, risk-everything love? Maybe he would have been thinking that . . . unless it was a passion like theirs, why fall in love? When you have their love affair as your model . . . wouldn't you want that?"

"Um . . . not if you ended up with your private parts cut off, August. I mean, that is not a happy ending."

"What if we could never—I mean not right now—but I'm talking *never* do it? Not ever? Could you still care about me?"

"Of course. There's more to you than that. Your mind, your personality."

"Exactly. Maybe Astrolabe was looking for his intellectual soul mate, as well as his physical soul mate. His parents had that physical passion, but then when that wasn't possible, they had this elevated intellectual passion."

I rolled back on my bed. "I wish I could just ask them. You know?"

"Instead, we have the book."

"We hope we have the book. We have to prove we have the book, that it was his."

"Will you kiss me on top of the Eiffel Tower?"

"Yes. Will you meet me at their tomb?"

"Yes, Calliope. Will you talk to me until I fall asleep?"

"Sure."

So we whispered about everything and nothing until long after I heard Harry and Gabe go to bed. I was certain August was my A.

15

Even when you are not here, I see your face as if in every passerby. —*A.*

We made plans to leave for Paris together in secret. Professor Sokolov and August contacted medieval scholars and monks in real monasteries, chasing leads long distance as to the origins of the Book of Hours. Uncle Harry used science and technology to analyze the vellum it was written on in an attempt to perfectly date the book. He also heard from a friend of his in London that the Tome Raider had supposedly been spotted in France but eluded the authorities once again.

Knowing that news of the Tome Raider would make everyone even more overprotective, we hid our plans. August's dad thought only August was going. And neither Harry nor Professor Sokolov had any idea of my plans. August and I decided I would phone Harry five minutes before I boarded and beg for him to understand.

For a week, I packed and unpacked in secret, wanting my wardrobe just right. I spent every waking minute with August, and every second we were apart, I felt sick to my stomach. I lost eight pounds just from not sleeping and living on coffee and feeling so excited that I couldn't eat. That and the ragged edges of guilt tugging at me.

The night before we were supposed to leave, Uncle Harry came into my room.

"I'm worried about you, Calliope."

"Why?"

"You look tired."

"I am."

"Love is supposed to be good for you."

"It is."

"I know. You can't sleep. You can't eat. You can't think. You can't do anything but think about August. I know. I've been there."

"With Gabe?"

"Oh, a little with him. But we were older when we met. We had jobs. We had respectable lives." He laughed. "The craziest thing I did was spend a small fortune on those tickets to his show over and over and over and over again."

"Yeah. You were just as bad."

"Maybe. But we still ate and slept. No, I was

insane in a younger love affair. In college. Then, I think I went months without sleeping. I was just so in love it was a sickness."

"Sleep is overrated."

"Look, I think young love is great. But summer will be over before you know it. I don't want you to fall apart when you have to go back to Boston. I know if you guys are meant to be, you'll work out the long-distance thing, and vacations, and everything. But an all-consuming passion isn't always healthy. I don't want you to get hurt. Okay?"

"You were the matchmaker," I said.

"I know, I know. I thought 'summer love.' I didn't think 'this is it' kind of love. Anyway, just . . . you know, humor your overprotective uncle just a tiny bit, okay?"

"Sure. Promise." And as soon as I said "promise," I regretted lying.

He looked at me skeptically and left my room. I knew I wouldn't do what he said. I felt like Heloise. How could anyone understand how I felt? Though August and I hadn't had sex, I knew I felt something for him passionately from deep inside.

I couldn't wait to go to Paris with him. He was the one.

August had paid for our tickets on a Sokolov and Sons credit card. I had eight hundred bucks cash, my spending money for the *entire* summer, and I took money from my savings account. I left Harry's while he was at work and Gabe was at the theater. August and I met at Penn Station and took the train to JFK airport.

It took us over an hour to get through security, but finally, we were at our gate. I looked at August. "Now or never."

I dialed Uncle Harry. I swallowed. My stomach twisted.

"Hello, Calliope."

"Harry . . . are you sitting down?"

"Oh, God . . . don't tell me you're pregnant!"

I hadn't thought that compared to that *news, Paris might seem tame!* "Actually, no. I'm on my way to Paris."

"WHAT?" I held the phone away from my ear slightly.

"We want to go to the tomb. We want to meet Etienne."

"I need a cocktail. You're lying. You cannot be doing this, Calliope."

"You were the one who sent us chasing the palimpsest. August and I are just finishing what we started."

"This is insane! Callie! Come back home right now. Where are you? I can hear flight announcements. I'm telling you—I'm *ordering* you."

"I'm not coming home, Harry. I'll be home in five days."

"The Tome Raider has been spotted by Interpol in Paris. Calliope, you need to come home."

"I'm not."

"This is . . . not acceptable. Your father . . . When your father finds out, he's going to kill me. Then you. He'll never let you stay with me again—Callie, how could you? This is the most selfish thing you have ever done."

"Uncle Harry . . ." I didn't know what else to say. He was right—I knew it. But I couldn't give in now. "Please, don't be mad."

"Calliope, for years, I have bragged to every person I know that my niece is level-headed, brilliant, a straight-A student, never gives me an ounce of trouble. Doesn't drink. Doesn't get into trouble. Friends told me *horror* stories of their teenagers. And I—*smugly*—said, 'Not me.' This is the most teenagery, impetuous, *stupid* thing you have ever done."

"Please," I was practically begging him. "Please try to understand."

August was squeezing my hand and trying to listen near my ear.

"Understand what?"

"Harry . . . Astrolabe's parents were like mine."

Harry was quiet. So I kept talking. "It's important to me to trace the book's origins. I was bitten by the history bug. You said so yourself. But it's more than that now. I have to do this for me. To prove something about myself."

There was a long silence.

"Harry?"

His voice was quiet. "How am I going to explain this to your dad?"

"I'll call him; you had nothing to do with this."

"No, I will. This is my fault. I filled your head with all this stuff. Thank goodness he has no idea what's at stake here. I'll book a flight to Paris and meet you two there. You can fill me in when I get there."

"Oh, Harry, thank you! Do you hate me?"

"I can't hate you, Calliope. But this, honest to God, would be something my sister would do. Though she'd probably get a tattoo first. You didn't get a tattoo, did you?"

"No." I laughed.

"I'll give you my travel arrangements as soon as I have them. Call me when you get there. And call me every step of the way. And be careful. Be very careful."

After we took off, August and I lifted the armrest between us, took one of the airline blankets, and I rested my head on his shoulder and fell asleep. All the nervous energy, the stress, the anxiety I felt when I was away from him evaporated. A calm settled through me, and I slept peacefully for hours.

When I woke up, August was still sleeping. I wriggled from his shoulder and maneuvered until his head rested on my lap and I could watch him sleep. His face was like a statue's, perfectly carved and beautiful, right to the way his upper lip rose like a cupid's bow. I watched dreams flit across his face as his eyes moved beneath their lids. He half smiled in his sleep.

I reached down and touched his cheek, then moved my hand to his hair. I wrapped strands around my fingers and thought my heart would just explode.

August woke up a short time later. I glanced across the aisle. Looking out the window, dawn was skittering across the sky in pinks and lavender. The flight attendants pushed a cart with coffee and pastries, and I ate and drank some coffee, then went to wash up and brush my teeth in the tiny airline bathroom.

I returned to my seat and waited for the plane to touch down in Paris. The City of Light.

We disembarked; my passport was stamped. *Bonjour!* We were that much closer to Heloise and Abelard and their final resting place.

We checked into our hotel. August had booked us into a quaint boutique hotel. Our room had two double beds, covered in old-fashioned-looking quilts, and wooden floors that creaked when we walked.

A small antique desk stood on one wall, facing a window. I crossed to it, and heavy linen paper stationery sat in a neat leather portfolio, as if waiting for me to write a letter. I stared out my window. If I stood on tiptoes, I could glimpse the Avenue des Champs-Élysées.

I showered and changed into the little black Barney's dress that Uncle Harry had bought for me. After pulling my hair into a soft ponytail, and putting on some lip gloss, I stepped out. August smiled. "The dress I first saw you in."

I nodded. *First* saw me in. That felt like something you would say after you were together a long time. *First* wasn't that long ago. But it felt like forever.

"It's my favorite. Come on, Etienne will be waiting."

We went to the lobby where a chauffeur waited, cap in hand. Etienne had hired us a car—which turned out to be a sleek black Mercedes—to take us to his antiquarian bookshop. We were finally going to meet Miriam's true love.

After a ten-minute ride in heavy Parisian traffic, we pulled up in front of the shop. Nestled on a side street, the store's bay front were windows filled with books and first editions that cost in the tens of thousands of dollars. It was filled with nooks and crannies, like a cluttered curiosity shop.

We rang a buzzer so he could let us in past the security alarm. I stepped inside, and August followed.

The old wooden floor creaked, not so different

from our hotel, and I stared upward. The ceiling had to be at least twenty feet high, and ladders on wheels rested up against shelves that lined every wall, stretching up with books as far as my eye could see.

"*Bonjour,*" Etienne greeted us. He shook August's hand then mine. He switched speaking to French-accented English. "Welcome my friends. Come, come. Welcome."

We followed him to the back of the store, passing tables filled with books. An antique couch, coffee table, and two chairs stood in a grouping.

"Sit, sit," he said. He looked just like in the pictures Miriam had shown us, his mustache perfectly trimmed, his suit elegant, his face handsome.

We sat down, and he offered us a plate of elaborate pastries. I was famished and took one. So did August. If I could have gotten away with taking two without looking rude, I would have.

"Tell me, first"—Etienne leaned forward, his face excited and pensive at the same time—"how is my friend, Miriam? Please tell me she is well."

I nodded. "We went to see her. She lives out on Long Island Sound now. And we ended up staying the night because of a horrible storm. She told us the whole story of the book."

I exchanged a glance with August. I wanted so

much to tell Etienne that I was certain Miriam still loved him. But I had to be certain he felt the same.

"Her home is beautiful," August offered. "She looks . . . at peace there."

"I am so glad to hear she is all right."

I nodded. "She showed us pictures from her time here, from the search for the book."

"I have pictures, too." Etienne jumped up, as if he had just been waiting for an excuse to retrieve them. He went to his desk and returned with a photo album and a picture in a frame that he clearly kept facing him while he worked.

"Here." He showed me the picture in a frame. "This is Miriam on a hill near the site of the original convent."

"It's beautiful," I whispered. Miriam was smiling at the camera, her face glowing and flushed with what looked like exertion on a summer day. Wind was clearly blowing her hair, and the sun shone on her—she wore a simple white sundress, and yet again I marveled how time hadn't dimmed her beauty at all.

August squeezed my hand. "She has a picture of you, too."

"Does she?" Etienne's eyes twinkled with pleasure.

I nodded. "I think she . . . misses you."

"Oh, how I miss her, too. You know, our search was the most exciting I have ever undertaken."

August leaned forward in his chair. "Did you know it was a palimpsest?"

Etienne shook his head. "You must understand, the book was nothing but a rumor. We thought, at most, at our greatest hope, that it had belonged to Heloise. That it had a connection to her as abbess. And so we paid a large sum to a dealer who said it came from a family—who wished to remain anonymous. Passed down through generations. There was some paperwork. I had no reason to doubt its truth but even so, I scrutinized. But Miriam needed to get it to New York. Perhaps it had been too easy. We were so excited, so enchanted by the book."

"But why the hurried sale? Wouldn't the palimpsest be worth so much more money if it had been verified?" August asked.

"Because, I fear, the dealer knew the book had been gotten by suspicious means. I believe he knew that if it had been verified as a palimpsest; it would not be allowed to leave the country, it would be a museum piece, for all the world to share. I believe the dealer was paid, that the entire transaction was orchestrated by thieves. Perhaps the dealer knew she would never take possession of it by less-than-

honorable measures. They knew Miriam was very,
very wealthy, but very, very honorable."

"Then where is the book from? You see—*We*
think . . ." I looked at August, who nodded. "We
think the book may have belonged to Heloise and
Abelard's son."

"Astrolabe? No!" Etienne jumped up, excited and
moving about like a nervous bird.

I nodded. "Yes. We think so, and it's so very
important to prove that, Etienne. We need to dig
deeper. We have to find out who was really behind
the book, who last owned it, and the person before
that and before that."

"Does Miriam know about this? About
Astrolabe?"

"Now she does," I said. I was willing him to
declare something more.

"I must speak to her."

"We have her number," August said eagerly.
"We're certain she would love to hear from you."

A cloud of doubt seemed to pass over Etienne's
eyes. "It has been some time since we last spoke. It
did not end well, our journey . . ."

"Time doesn't matter with someone like Miriam,"
I offered. "Think of Heloise and Abelard. They went
twelve years without communicating."

"I ... She was very wealthy." He faced a bookshelf and rested his hand, as if composing himself. "Married. I had no hope of ..." He turned to look at us. "I would like to hear her voice, after so many years. Do you think it is possible?"

I nodded. "Call her."

"I will tell you more about the book, but this I must do right now. Will you excuse me, my new friends?"

"Of course," I said. August looked up Miriam's number on his BlackBerry and handed it to Etienne, who went into his office while we waited.

As soon as he was gone, I took a second pastry. "I am so hungry!"

I happily ate flaky French pastries filled with cream and fresh raspberries. We waited and Eitenne returned about twenty minutes later, beaming. "My friends! She is coming to Paris."

I clapped my hands with delight.

Etienne sat. "I am as happy as a schoolboy. Now the book."

August nodded.

"For this, we go see the other dealer. His store is in Nantes. It is four hours by car. I will make arrangements, but you must be careful. We mustn't reveal what our trip is about. I will simply say I have some American buyers perhaps interested in his first editions—he specializes in religious texts. Thus, he had the Book of Hours."

He walked to the phone on his desk, placed a call, and spoke rapidly in French. He nodded several times, then hung up.

"We go by car tomorrow morning. We will find the origins of this most special book. We will do all this for Miriam. She will be very happy to know, *non*?"

"*Oui*," August said. "Very happy."

We left Etienne's bookstore after agreeing to meet him for dinner that night. We spent the rest of the day wandering Paris. We made our way to the Eiffel Tower, and we strolled, hand in hand.

The streets, the whole city, felt so ancient compared to Manhattan, which always felt, to me, like a place built in a rush of skyscrapers. My favorite places in New York had always been those with older buildings—neighborhoods like Tudor City—where you could imagine more history. Maybe, I mused, I'd been bitten by the history bug long ago.

"Remember your promise," August said, leaning over to kiss my neck.

"A kiss on the top of the Eiffel Tower."

When we reached the tower itself, there was a long line of tourists waiting to go up to the top. And there we encountered a hitch to our plan.

"August . . . there's no way to go to the top without getting in an elevator."

I watched the color draining from his cheeks. "What?"

"The stairs go to the second floor. But that's it."

He let go of my hand and began pacing. "You know, I wouldn't blame you if you . . . I know, I know, I'm a little like him. My dad. I try not to be, but I am."

Just then my cell phone rang. It was my father. I exhaled. This *so* wasn't going to go well.

"Calliope!"

I winced. "Yes, Dad?"

"So we finally settle things, finally have a conversation—a real conversation—and this is how you repay me."

"*Repay* you? I'll admit that this was maybe the most . . . crazy thing I've ever done, but I don't owe you for you finally answering questions about my mother."

"I could have that boy arrrested."

"Dad, don't . . . Mom is the reason I'm here."

"Your mother has nothing to do with this crazy scheme."

"I know you don't understand, but she would. I want to leave a letter at the tomb of Heloise and Abelard."

"Calliope, this is a serious, serious breach of trust."

I could practically feel the rage in his voice. I was very glad there was an ocean between us.

"I know," I said softly. "But for once, trust that I know what I'm doing. Without you planning out my whole future for me."

"Harry assured me he would come and retrieve you." He was talking over me. Ignoring my end of the conversation.

"You're not listening to me again."

"Calliope . . . You are lucky it's not me coming over to get you. And when you get home, there *will* be consequences."

"I know. Dad, please. Just try to understand. Remember how you felt when you saw my mother?"

"You're too young to feel like that—"

"You can't make me *not* feel like that." I cut him off. "And calling August 'that boy' isn't going to make him go away."

"I have to go into a meeting, but we will continue this discussion at a later time."

"Fine."

I ended the call. Of course he had to go into a meeting. I'd never heard him so furious, but what did I expect? I looked at August, who was shaking his head.

"Between my neuroses, and me getting you in trouble—"

"*I* made the decision to go." Just like Heloise.

August looked up at the Eiffel Tower.

"It's all right," I said. "We don't have to go to the top."

"But we promised to. It would be bad luck to break the promise."

"Well, it's not like we can climb to the top. It's the elevator or nothing."

He looked at me with real fear in his eyes. "We have to go to the top."

"Can you?" I hugged him tightly. "It won't be any fun if you're up there half terrified."

"No. I'm doing it. You came all this way to go up there, and from what I could hear of that call...you are in *so* much trouble. No...I'm doing it."

Face resolute, he grabbed me by the hand, and we stood in line. I could see him tensing each time the yellow elevator doors opened and people poured out, and then people boarded, and we inched forward bit by bit. A variety of languages filled the air— French, Spanish, German, English, and I heard what sounded to me like the accented English of Australia, Scotland, and Ireland.

"August," I said firmly, "we really and truly do not have to do this."

"We do."

Finally, we were near the front of the line. He was clenching and unclenching his jaw. I reached up with my free hand to stroke his face. "I love you even if we don't get to the top."

The doors opened and the last passengers climbed off. Almost as if the crowd was a living creature, we were pushed slightly, like an amoeba moving along, into the elevator. I wrapped my arms around August's neck.

"Look at me," I whispered. "Only me. Nothing else."

August looked in my eyes. The elevator doors closed, and we started moving up. His breathing was shallow, so I said, "Breathe with me."

I slowed my breathing, and I stared at him with all the love I could show him. And before we knew it, we were at the top. The doors opened. We stepped off.

He looked around in amazement. "I did it, Calliope."

"I'm proud of you."

"Promises must be kept," he said, then he bent me over backward in a dip and kissed me full on my mouth. When he raised me up again, he said, "Now we'll never be parted. It's the City of Love, the City of Light. Our promise is sealed."

I hugged him, and we walked and stared down on Paris, her streets and the river laid out before us like a picture postcard.

"I never want to go home," I murmured. "Wouldn't it be great to live here, even for six months or a year? Study here?"

"Yeah. Maybe someday we can."

We stood on the deck of the Eiffel Tower for a long time, not saying anything. The air in Paris, I decided, was more romantic than at home. And I wanted to breathe in every bit of the city's love and August's.

I wanted our kiss on the top of the Eiffel Tower to mean forever.

16

My secrets are as deep as a mountain valley.
—*A.*

That night, I dreamed of Heloise.

She was young—my age—but already a nun, dressed in a white habit, and sitting at a plain wooden desk beneath a small window composing a letter. I was invisible, there in her room, which had stone floors and little gray light, a plain bed with a straw mattress. She shivered in the chilly dawn, a small candle lighting her words.

I peered over her shoulder. Her script was neat, each letter perfectly aligned in height to the letter next to it.

My Darling Astrolabe,

All of the world knows of the sin of thy mother and thy father, speaking of the wages of our love, the price extracted for my unchaste nature. Thou, dear child, are an evidence even the most vehement of denials cannot hide. No stomach burst with love's greatest rose can be hidden from the eyes of the whole of the earth.

My child, 'tis best for thou to be apart, raised in the bosom of a family of reputation worthy of an innocent.

Cast your eyes, my Astrolabe, not on the stars of Heaven, but on the Son of Heaven. Do not be tempted by lips nor hair nor face so fair. Do not make the mistakes of thy parents.

I sign this as thy mother, and as thy example of a woman fallen now given up to God in penance, the wife of thy father, yet not his wife.

H.

Heloise's face was unlined, but her eyes were sad. She touched her breast, as if writing the words pained her. Suddenly, Heloise looked up at me, and she was transformed into my mother. And then I woke up.

I sat up in bed and could see by the sky that it was the middle of the night. I tried to shake off the dream. But it lingered.

I looked over at August, who slept in the other bed in sweatpants and a T-shirt, undisturbed, unaware of my dream. I slipped from my own bed and went to the window to look out at Paris. August and I had decided we wouldn't have sex yet—I wasn't ready—but even being in the same room at night was awesome, whispering in the dark until we fell asleep.

Harry was arriving in a day. I had spoken to Gabe, and he said after two stiff martinis—something Harry rarely, if ever, drank—he had calmed down enough to phone my father. According to Gabe, there was considerable yelling, but then some sort of truce. I hoped I could forge my own truce with my dad over this.

Paris was as romantic as I had hoped, but I wanted to find the path of Heloise. I sat in the small chintz chair in the corner, and sometime in the night, I fell back to sleep.

After a restless few hours, I woke again. My cell phone rang, and it was Etienne telling me that August and I had time for café au lait and croissants before the drive to Nantes, since he was stuck in traffic.

I woke August, and we got ready. We met Etienne in the lobby. He drove us in his BMW. August sat up front, and I rode in the back, occasionally drifting off to sleep; each time I woke, the scenery was spectacular and unlike any place I had been before.

The previous night, over dinner, Etienne had taken us through what he knew. Miriam had bought several books and items from him over the years, and they had a warm correspondence, but she was most interested in a Book of Hours. As he searched, a monk had told him of a rumor that a Book of Hours had survived from Heloise's convent, which had been forced to scatter. Whether this book was fake or real, the monk had no idea. There was always a chance of forgery, but still, Etienne felt it was worth pursuing.

In the front seat, August stared out the window.

"What's wrong?" I asked him.

"You wouldn't believe me if I told you."

"Of course I would."

He leaned over the backseat to talk more softly. "Last night, Abelard came to me in a dream."

I swear the car got twenty degrees colder.

"What?"

He nodded and whispered. "He came to me, and the dream was as real as you and me, Calliope. I mean, if I didn't know any better, I would say a ghost visited me."

"Heloise visited *me* last night."

He stared at me. "What happened in your dream?"

"She was writing a letter to Astrolabe, and she let me read it. What happened in your dream?"

"He was saying prayers, reading from a Book of Hours. I went and knelt down next to him, and when

I looked at the book, it was A.'s. I could read some of the lines we know, like the one from Genesis. All of a sudden, he grabbed my hand—tight. I tried to pull away, but he was tugging on me, and he said, 'Find her.'"

"Find her? Who? Heloise?"

"I don't know. I thought so, but I don't know. He was really distraught. He was crying."

Even though the day was sunny, I was chilly. It seemed like from the across the centuries, ghosts were leading us on this chase.

We drove on for a couple of hours until we came to Nantes. My breath caught. The city was beautiful. A port town, old schooners rested in its waters, their tall masts reflected on the blueness on the clear day. A cathedral stood guard over the city's inhabitants, its spires rising to the heavens. I hoped Nantes, with its verdant lawns next to courtyards and old buildings, would lead us a step closer to the son Heloise had to give up.

Etienne parked the car next to a shop, and we climbed out. Like his own location, this one had elaborate security, and we waited to be buzzed in.

Once inside, though, any resemblance to Etienne's shop was gone. This one was cold and modern inside, with marble floors and glass cases containing illuminated manuscripts. I saw August's eyes scanning the array of ancient treasures.

The book dealer, a portly man in a starched white shirt, black pants, and a pair of paisley suspenders, greeted us and began speaking rapidly to Etienne in French. Occasionally, I made out the words *manuscrit* and *livre*.

Etienne, who was the picture of a gentleman the day before and at dinner the night before, suddenly grew angry. His voice rose, and he started talking with his hands. He inched closer to the other man, until they were almost nose to nose.

The book dealer turned his backs to us and slammed his hand down on a counter—I thought the glass would shatter.

Etienne crossed his arms and stood his ground. The book dealer stared at Etienne. It reminded me of the playground staring contests when I was a kid.

The book dealer blinked first. He threw his hands up, rolled his eyes, and stormed to a back room. When he returned, he handed Etienne a piece of paper.

Etienne took it and, face impassive, motioned for us to follow him out.

Once out on the street, we climbed in the car and he drove to the port. "Come, we walk and talk," he said as he put the car in park.

Climbing out again, we stood with him at the water's edge, hearing the waves lapping at the dock.

"Voilà!" Etienne said, and turned the paper around.

"Abbé Bruno?" I read the name aloud.

"*Oui!*"

"And who is Abbé Bruno," August asked.

"The abbott who will lead us to the truth. Tomorrow, we depart."

Etienne strolled in the sun, a look of satisfaction on his face, after having stared down the dealer.

"It was as I suspected. At some point in history, the manuscript was stolen. This man the dealer supposedly bought the manuscript from had manufactured a provenance. And when Miriam and I wanted to check further, her husband, Monsieur Rose, was in such a rush to acquire, he didn't care what was forged. He wanted to possess it."

"But he never cared about Heloise," I said. "Miriam did."

August raised his index finger. "Ah, but we know Rose was a collector. He wanted to own it simply to own it. That was how he was with everything in his life."

"Precisely, my American friend. So this abbott—he knows, supposedly, more than anyone about Heloise and Abelard. And he has a story to tell. And tomorrow . . . we go to hear it. Face-to-face. *C'est bon*."

"Harry will be here in the morning. My uncle. He will come with us."

I squeezed August's hand. We were close, so close to history. So close to Heloise and Abelard and Astrolabe. They were all around us. I felt it. I dreamed it.

August dreamed it.

They needed us.

That night, August and I had a romantic dinner at a place on the Seine.

I dressed in a black miniskirt, a black sleeveless turtleneck, and my most favorite shawl, which Gabe had bought me one Christmas. It's pashmina, in a deep shade of green, with beading on the fringe.

"You look gorgeous," August said as he greeted me. He had gone for a walk to buy me a rose.

"You look handsome yourself," I said, walking across the lobby to kiss him.

He grabbed me by the hand, and we strode out into the night air.

After dinner we walked along the Seine, and it felt like I had somehow stepped into a movie.

When we returned to the hotel, we rode up in the elevator together. When we got to our room, I slipped off my heels.

"Calliope, I found out something really cool."

"What?"

"I found out that at the cemetery where they are buried, if you are single, you write a letter to Heloise and Abelard, asking them to find you a soul mate. But if you already are with your true love, you each leave a letter by their tomb, professing your love. So just before closing on Saturday let's go there, where they are . . . with letters, and leave them there for Heloise and Abelard."

I looked at him. "My dad and mom did that. And look how *that* turned out." At the thought of my dad, my stomach clenched a little.

"Come on, we're not them. We're different."

"All right. But . . . what do we write exactly?"

"What's in your heart." He kissed me.

I looked into his eyes. I wasn't sure exactly how to explain everything that was in my heart. How do you explain feeling like you were meant to be with someone? As if history and a book and ghosts and dreams were bringing you together?

17

To whom do we take our vows? —A.

The next day, Harry finally arrived. He then marched me and my suitcase to *his* room and said he would stay with August. It wasn't like I could argue with him. However, he barely had time to set his suitcase in his room before we took the train to Avignon, where we were to meet Abbé Bruno at the monastery where he lived and worked. We were to stay overnight on the monastery grounds, and Harry, Etienne, August, and I each brought a small overnight bag.

Harry sulked at me for about fifteen minutes, but when we told him about our dreams, he said, "All right, I give in. Maybe this is bigger than all of us."

The train ride passed from the bustle of Paris. For over two hours, we sped through France, to the bucolic Avignon countryside. A three-arched bridge spanned a river as calm as glass.

We disembarked at the station, and Etienne arranged for a car and driver to take us a couple of miles up steep country roads to a monastery on a hillside.

"This monastery," Etienne said, "makes its own bread—very famous, actually. And wine. They take orders from as far away as America for their wine."

I gazed up the mountain as the car completed its climb.

"Laypeople may come here to stay as a retreat. I believe they have thirty beds."

The driver pulled onto a wide dirt drive, between two stone pillars, until at last we were outside the Gothic-style castle monastery. Two spires with needlelike points rose up. Windows seemed to peer out from stone like silent sentinels guarding the gardens surrounding the castle, with rows of yew hedges forming a green wall around it.

I climbed from the car and took August's hand as Harry and Etienne led the way to the massive wooden door, which stood twenty or twenty-five feet high.

Etienne pressed a button, which made a sound like an ancient bell. A voice spoke out from an intercom, and Etienne replied in French.

After he spoke, he said to Harry and us, "We will be shown in."

A short time later, the door swung open and a plump elderly woman in a simple housecoat and apron motioned us in, identifying herself as the monastery's housekeeper. She led us into a huge hallway the size of a ballroom in width, with marble-slab tiles and a ceiling as high as a cathedral's.

My shoes echoed as we walked along the stone floors. Simple beeswax candles burned in sconces on the wall, for though it was midday, the interior was dim because the massive hallway had only one set of windows at the far end.

The housekeeper stopped at a doorway. Next to it was a simple brass plaque. ABBÉ BRUNO.

She knocked, and a booming voice called out, *"Entré!"*

The housekeeper bowed her head as the four of us entered Abbé Bruno's office.

The man sitting at the immense wooden desk had the appearance of Santa Claus, with a thick white beard and white hair, though his circled a bald pate. He had on simple brown robes and a white collar, and when he stood to shake our hands, I saw he wore plain brown sandals.

Etienne made introductions, and Abbé Bruno gestured to chairs and two couches that circled a huge stone fireplace on the other side of his office.

He moved from behind his desk and lumbered over, rocking slightly from side to side as he walked, and huffing out of breath.

He didn't so much sit in his chair as collapse into it.

"Well . . . I will speak English. Maybe not so well. You have come about Heloise *et* Peter Abelard, *non*?"

Harry nodded. He explained about the book, the auction, his position with the auction house, and the belief, tentatively forming and growing stronger, that A. might be Astrolabe.

Abbé Bruno listened to Harry, joining his index fingers beneath his chin and nodding from time to time. When Harry finished talking, Abbé Bruno didn't say anything for some time.

Finally, he whispered, "I have a story to tell of Heloise."

I leaned forward on the couch, feeling the hair at my nape rise.

"Before she was abbess of the Paraclete, she was a prioress at Argenteuil. But she and the nuns were turned out—their order would have scattered."

"Why were they turned out?" I asked.

"Oh . . ." He laughed. "The monks wanted their convent space, in a matter of simplifying things. Abelard's monks wanted the convent. So then he arranged for her to go to the Paraclete, where she became abbess. Now, going back in time, one of the monks of this order of Abelard had a sister who was a nun at the Paraclete.

Harry shook his head. "It's always fascinating to me how old history is here, when we upstarts in America have only been around for two hundred and twenty-five years or so. Give or take."

Abbé Bruno laughed, slapping his belly. "Yes. We have stone in this building placed a thousand years ago . . . And so it was that, through history, we possessed what some of us thought was a manuscript from the Paraclete. Passed from sister nun to sister nun, to brother monk to brother monk. Through time."

"Was the manuscript Heloise's?" Harry asked. "The Book of Hours? Was it hers?"

He raised a finger. "Ah, we might think so. But here's the mystery. During World War II, we were occupied by the Nazis. And at that point, the Book of Hours disappeared."

Etienne gasped. "You mean?"

"Indeed," said Abbé Bruno. "If you possess the manuscript, it was likely stolen by the Nazis." He spat the word. "From there, you know, anything could have happened to it."

Harry leaned back and studied Abbé Bruno skeptically.

"I see how your mind works, my clever man." Abbé Bruno wagged a finger as thick as a sausage at Harry. "I was too young to have seen the manuscript with my own eyes. Avignon was freed from Nazi control in August 1944. I was just a tiny boy—three years old. I had not yet heard the gentle knocking on the door of my heart of my Father in heaven, telling me to dedicate my life in service to him."

"Do you know anyone who saw it? Anyone who is still here?" Harry asked. "We need to have hard proof."

"Brother Pietro, he is eighty-five. He saw it. Still has all his faculties intact."

I looked at August. This was it. The realization of all we had done this summer, of it all. The trip to Miriam's, the trip over the ocean, the research and digging, all the work Harry and Professor Sokolov had done.

"Can we talk to him?" August asked.

"I will arrange it. He works, still, in the kitchens, baking bread. I will ask that he come to my office. In the meantime, I will have our housekeeper bring us some warm bread, some cheese from the farmer up the road, and perhaps a bottle of wine for us adults, *non*?"

"Oui!" Harry agreed.

Father Pietro was as hunched and thin as Abbé Bruno was round and jolly. He shuffled into the office as we were finishing our cheese and bread.

Abbé Bruno helped him into a soft chair, and he spoke French in a tremulous voice. Abbé Bruno translated for us, slowly.

"I hear . . . you want to know about the book."

"We do," Harry said softly. "Very much so. We've come all the way from New York City to ask about the Book of Hours."

"I have seen it. One time."

My heart fell a little. One time. Over sixty years ago. How could he possibly remember?

"The war made things very difficult. I had never been anywhere except my father's small farm. When my father died, I worked the farm. Then the Nazis came. And my mother and sister were killed in a bomb. I was all alone, starving, frightened. But the brothers here took me in."

He stopped and shut his eyes. I thought he was

falling asleep, but he opened them again, the whites of his eyes rheumy and moist, and continued. "I did any job that needed doing. I swept the floors, and I made soup in the kitchen. It was wartime—there were no eggs, no meat. We ate a lot of watery soup. Some bread. Anything good—any meats or fresh vegetables—went to feed the Nazis."

I listened to history unfolding before me.

"The Nazis, they did not respect the churches here. They did not respect women and children. They did not respect the old people. They did not care that people were hungry and dying. We began to fear that they would overrun this very monastery, that we would have to protect it from them. And then one day Brother Simeon came to me."

The old monk's voice lowered further, as if he was still keeping this secret, sixty years later.

"He said that the monastery was the hiding place for a very special Book of Hours. He told me it was passed from a sister in the order of Paracletes to her brother, a Dominican monk. And so it was passed, from brother to brother to sister to brother, for safekeeping."

"Did he tell you it was Heloise's?" I asked. Abbé Bruno translated, and the old monk nodded.

"He said it belonged to the wife of Peter Abelard.

And that she was a nun. I did not know the story then. I knew the name of Abelard, but that was it. I was not a scholar here; I was just a boy. I knew the book was special."

August asked, "Did you see it?"

"I did. He showed me. I was a young boy from a farm. I had never seen anything so beautiful in all my life. He had it wrapped in five pieces of woven cloth to protect it. He unwrapped one, then the other, then the other. Finally, he showed me the book. The pages were edged with gold. I think it was real gold. And the lettering was so neat. At the time, I could only write my name. So even though I could not read the letters, I could tell they were written with great love. Great care. Each one the same height as the letter next to it."

Harry leaned very close to the old man. "This is very important. Do you remember what the picture was on the first page? Do you remember anything about it?"

"I remember two things. One, that there was a beautiful pheasant on one page. I had never seen anything so beautiful, each feather painted and colorful. It looked, I thought, like a real pheasant."

"And the other?" August urged.

"Brother Simeon showed me two pages. On one was a man, kneeling, by a harp. The other, on the face page, was a woman with a halo around her head. She was supposed to be the Blessed Mother."

"Supposed to be?" August asked.

The old man leaned toward us and showed us his two hands, then pressed them together—palm to palm.

"The man with the harp was Abelard. The woman—she was not the Blessed Mother. It was a likeness of Heloise. Pressed together, they were one, for eternity. Together in the book."

I felt as if every single nerve was on fire. "Uncle Harry, do you know if those two pages are in the book?"

He shook his head. "I'll call New York, but honestly, I've been through it over and over again, and this image is not ringing a bell."

"No," I jumped up. "It has to be the book. We've come all this way."

Abbé Bruno looked equally disappointed. "We were hoping to get our book back. To honor it. A museum piece. A part of our history lost to the Nazis."

"I'm sorry," Uncle Harry said.

Etienne, too, looked devastated. "I do not recall those pages, either, when Miriam and I saw it. I'm so sorry. Abbé Bruno, Brother Pietro, you have been so generous with your time."

Dejectedly, we stood, ready to leave.

Abbé Bruno said, "Do not give up your search. Sometimes, the most wonderful of blessings is around the next corner, merely hidden from view. Romans eight, verse twenty-eight, 'And we know that all things work together for good to them that love God, to them who are called according to his purpose.'"

I nodded, trying not to cry, trying to conceal how much my heart hurt at that moment. If it wasn't the book, then August's and my dreams were just made up. We were kidding ourselves that fate had brought us together, fate and ghosts. Instead, we were just two people who really liked each other. Nothing more. Nothing less. And certainly nothing mystical.

The housekeeper came to show us to our rooms. Mine was separate from the men's, on a different floor. It was as spartan as I imagined Heloise's might have been, with a simple wooden bed frame, constructed from unpolished wood and roughly hewn together, covered by a thin mattress. A plain white coverlet and white sheets adorned it. A wooden crucifix hung on the wall above the headboard. Next to the bed, a simple wooden table, again unpolished, served as a nightstand. On it sat a Bible in French. A small scatter rug covered the floor by the bed. It looked woven of simple rags.

No radio. No TV. No mirror. One outlet on the stone wall, and a small armoire to hang clothes. A single lamp with a plain shade stood on the night table. A single, small window that overlooked a courtyard, was high on the wall—above my head.

At dinner that night, Etienne, Harry, August, and I were positively depressed. None of us spoke. When it came time to say good night, August barely looked at me or acknowledged me. It hurt, not even having the comfort of him next to me.

After dinner, we had little choice. We each went to our simple rooms. Sun set, plunging the castle into darkness, save for the weak beams of my lamp. I washed in the bathroom across the hall from my room and went back into my room and changed into sweatpants and a T-shirt for bed. With nothing to do, I decided to work on my letter to August for the night we were to go to the tomb.

I had brought hotel stationery with me. But each time I tried to start the letter, I hated what I wrote. I kept writing, scratching out, writing, and scratching out. Finally, I crumbled the paper, and feeling tears in my eyes, scrunched down into bed and soon fell into a fitful sleep.

18

What secrets come in dreams of my beloved?
                                          —A.

I dreamed again of Heloise. She woke me up, touching my shoulder.

"Hush, child," she said, her finger to her lips. "Follow me."

I obeyed, rising from my bed and pulling on a robe against the chill. My room no longer had a lamp, or a plug, or even my suitcase or a mattress. Instead, a straw pallet sat on wooden platform. Moonlight shone into the room, illuminating Heloise. Her face was beautiful, unlined, her skin pale and luminous, her eyes bright and clear.

The floor, icy beneath my feet, woke me up fully. I shivered. This wasn't a dream.

Heloise, dressed in a plain nightgown with a nightcap, tiptoed into the hallway and looked left and right. Then she carefully crept to the small chapel downstairs.

"Come," she beckoned me.

I followed her, trying to keep up, terrified of the dark, because I could only follow the glow of her single candle as it appeared to dance like a ghost down the hall. I was afraid to look away from the apparition, and afraid that I was imagining it.

She stopped at a door far down the hall, then quietly pushed on it and slipped inside. Not wanting to be left alone in the darkness, I scurried to where she had just been, opened the door, heart thumping, and crept into the blackness.

I didn't know where I was, but it felt like a tomb. The room was suffocatingly black, and I couldn't see Heloise or the candlelight. I looked around, not even able to spy my own hand. But then I saw a flicker on a wall. She was back by an altar. I was in a chapel.

Barefoot, I padded down the center aisle until I reached the altar.

Heloise pointed at a statue. I crept closer. It was the Virgin Mary. But I could see Heloise pointed more insistently at a single stone.

Puzzled, I reached out to touch it. But then Heloise looked over her shoulder in fear. Out in the hallway I heard boots. Footsteps. Lots of them.

I hurriedly ran to the door and opened it a sliver. Nazis were everywhere. I heard them shouting, and their steps were loud and echoing and terrifying. I heard one of them coming, so I ducked in a pew, then hid underneath it, flattening myself to the cold floor. I was afraid to breathe. The Nazis raised lanterns. My heart pounded so hard, I thought its beating would give me away. A pair of black boots stopped by the bench. I swore I could see my own reflection in the shine of the boots. Praying, I whispered internally, "Please, don't let them see me."

I was grateful when the boots moved, retreated, and Heloise and I were in silence again.

I crept from my hiding spot and stood, aching from the cold floor.

"Heloise?" I called out. I couldn't see her, or her candle.

Desperate to find my ghost again, I left the chapel and was still in darkness out in the hallway. From behind me, I heard a voice shout, "There! A girl! Stop!"

Nazis ran down the hall, and I turned and fled, my feet cold and scraped as I found the staircase, and tripped. I fell, and one of the soldiers grabbed my shoulder roughly.

"You!" He screamed at me.

And then, I woke up.

19

We lie forever, married for eternity. —*A.*

I sat up in bed. I was in my room. Gratefully, I flicked on the light. I look at my hands and saw they were trembling. When I shut my eyes, I could see the German soldier grabbing me. I could feel it. I was positive what had happened to me had been real, but there I was underneath the covers.

I looked at my watch. It was three A.M. I had to get into the chapel. I was certain that somehow the ghost of Heloise was telling me something. That statue? The stone? Something.

I climbed from bed. My bare feet on the stone reminded me of the dream. It was just as cold as it had been.

I fumbled through my bag for a pair of socks and pulled them on. Afraid of being caught, I opened my door just a crack. No on was in the hallway.

Because the monastery now operated as a retreat house, the hallways had small sconces lit for people needing to use the bathrooms at night. The lights were pale and flickering, but I could at least see.

Tiptoeing, I hurried down the hall, praying no one would be up and around. I knew the brothers woke early—before dawn—for prayer, but I thought that wouldn't be for another hour or so.

I ran down the central staircase, a sweeping wide marble creation with a mahogany banister. At the bottom, I turned left and headed to the chapel.

I pressed on the door. Inside, it was pitch-black, so I fumbled on the wall for a light of some sort, found a switch, and flicked it. A wooden chandelier lit, casting illumination on the hard wooden pews, the simple altar, and the statue of Mary to the left of the altar—just as in my dream. It couldn't be. I was positive that I had not been in this chapel before. Not even on the short tour we had been given.

I ran to the statue. The face of the Mary statue was serene, carved of marble, and white.

I crossed myself in a sign of deference. "I need to know what's hidden here; I need to find Heloise's book. Can you help me?" I beseeched the statue. "Please?"

Behind me, I heard someone at the door. I withdrew behind the statue—until I saw it was August.

"August! What are you doing here?" I whispered.

"Abelard . . . he came to me again. In a dream."

"Heloise came to me in mine," I whispered, feeling like a spider was crawling up my spine.

"He showed me something. Something hidden."

"Was it here? Behind a stone, by the statue?"

"Yes, I think so. But it was dark . . . I don't know."

I looked around the statue's base, but I didn't see anything that made sense to me as far as a secret. The two of us ran our fingers along the marble, the folds of Mary's dress soft—the marble perfectly smooth.

I knelt down. Heloise had pointed to a stone. I ran my fingers along the wall beneath the statue. I saw no special lettering, nothing that would mean anything in my search.

My heart still throbbed. There had to be something. The chapel was just as I had dreamed it. Heloise was trying to tell me something.

"Do you remember your dream?" I asked him.

"Like it was real. Really happening."

"Let's each of us just concentrate."

I shut my eyes and relived the dream, scary as it was.

Then I remembered. A stone had seemed to glow.

I opened my eyes again, only this time, they gravitated toward one particular stone. I looked at August. He was pointing at the same stone.

We moved to it, hurriedly, frantically, touching it. Still nothing. Then I moved my fingers along the sides. One corner had a chip. I poked the edge of my finger into the chipped corner and could feel the stone shift slightly.

"Oh, Heloise," I whispered aloud. I pulled on the stone. It came loose. And there, beneath the marble statue of Mary, I found a secret cache.

I reached my hand into the darkness, praying no rats were in there. My fingers felt along sandy gravel, and then stopped. I felt something solid. Grabbing it, I withdrew the box.

"Oh, God, August," I breathed. "This could be it. Could be what our entire search was for."

He swallowed. "The find of a lifetime."

Pulling the box into the dim light, I saw it was covered with burlap cloth, and dusty. I blew on it. Unwrapping gingerly, the box was wooden and carved.

Heloise et Abelard

My mouth went completely dry.

My hands shook. "I can't," I whispered. "You do it."

Carefully, he opened the tiny latch. And there,

nestled on velvet, were two perfectly preserved leaves of manuscript.

Heloise and Abelard. The man with the harp, the woman with the halo.

Together for eternity.

20

You are lost to me, and each day I weep and gnash my teeth. —*A.*

"Miss Calliope?" Abbé Bruno entered the chapel, eyes widening when he found me there, tears streaming down my face, hugging August.

"Look, Abbé! Look what we found."

He rushed to my side, and as soon as he saw the pages, his eyes welled. "But how?"

In a rush of words, it all came tumbling out—the dream, the rock, the chipped corner, how it moved.

Abbé Bruno crossed himself three times and genuflected at the cross. When two brothers came into the chapel for morning prayers, Abbé Bruno instead sent them to get Harry and Etienne so we could share the good news.

Harry arrived first, running at full speed to the pages, which we had gingerly placed on the altar.

"I don't believe it," he whispered.

"I dreamed it was here, Harry. I *dreamed* it."

"What?"

I repeated the story. He kept shaking his head. He looked from me, to August, to the hole in the stone wall, to me, to August again.

He leaned in close as Etienne arrived, and together they examined the edges.

"Look how clean the edge is here, where it would have been bound into the manuscript," Harry said. "Someone cut it from the book. Perhaps they knew these were the most important pages. They wanted to make sure Heloise and Abelard were together."

"But why not hide the whole book?" Etienne asked.

"Look at the hole," I said. "It wouldn't be large enough for the thickness of the manuscript. And maybe whoever it was hoped that if the Nazis had no idea of the importance of the Book of Hours, they would just . . . I don't know . . . leave it alone."

Harry could barely contain himself. "I need to call the director of the auction house immediately! I'm going outside where my phone will have better reception."

"James Rose will never let it be auctioned off now," I said. "He'll pull it."

Harry smiled. "It doesn't matter. Now that there's

proof, the book will be returned to its rightful heirs.
The monastery, the brothers."

At that moment, I loved Uncle Harry so much.
He'd lost his commission and was happy about it.
It was about *history* for him, and not about money.

"I must call Miriam," Etienne said.

"We'll leave you to morning prayers, Abbé
Bruno," Harry said.

August and I walked the hall. "Can you explain to
me what just happened?" I whispered.

"No."

"It *did* just happen, though, right?"

"Yeah, but it makes no sense. It's as if they really
did come to us, to me and you, and chose us."

We found Uncle Harry outside. He was on the
phone and I paced and waited. He said, "All right,
Gabe. Love you. Calliope sends love, too."

I nodded in agreement. Then he hung up.

"You look like you've seen a ghost."

"August and I still can't believe it. Do you believe
in ghosts?"

"I do. But you know, I've always been a little
weird that way. Maybe you two are reincarnated.
Or maybe..." His voice trailed off.

"Maybe what?" I asked.

"Maybe you both needed to believe in the book more than anyone else. Maybe, in some way, you willed this whole miracle into being."

"Can we go back to Paris now? We need to go to their tomb. We need to tell them."

"Honey, we have to make arrangements for the pages. They need to be taken to New York, reunited with the manuscript, and then, if we can prove the Book of Hours was stolen by the Nazis, the monastery can get the book back. We have to cross the t's and dot the i's before this is all over. The Tome Raider . . . I bet you he was involved somehow."

"Miriam loves the book, but you know, she'll just be happy it's where it's supposed to be."

"Exactly. So we're going to be here for a little while yet. Try to relax. I'm sure there's a logical explanation for how you found it." He looked from August to me. "Or not."

August and I walked out on the monastery grounds in silence. Maybe Harry was right. Maybe we needed the book more than anyone else.

21

When love is gone, a hollow remains, like the space in Adam's ribs where Eve was formed.
—A.

On Saturday, we got ready to go to the cemetery. After telling Harry and Etienne our plans, we all worked on letters. I wrote mine, imagining Heloise standing like an angel over my shoulder, whispering her guidance.

> Dear August,
>
> I can't explain what happened at the monastery, but I have felt as if Heloise and Abelard have somehow guided us from the moment we met. I know that doesn't even make sense, since we only met this summer, but from that first moment in your little greenhouse, I have lived and breathed as if you were my soul mate.
>
> I feel like Heloise has been my guardian angel. She led me to the pages. And all along, she led me

to you. Beneath her Book of Hours, I am positive those are the hidden words of Astrolabe, the child of a burning love story. Somehow, it seemed fitting to me, this child of a mother destroyed by love, to find you, to find love, because of Astrolabe.

We are supposed to leave letters pledging eternal love. I pledge that because I know that somehow we are different from our parents. We're different even from Heloise and Abelard. We are like them, but we will never do what they did. We will never destroy each other.

Eternity is a long time. But no matter what happens, I will always have the dreams of Heloise. I will always have our adventure. The palimpsest. The whispered words of a secret manuscript. You will always be my first love. My true love. My A.

Love,
Calliope

I folded the pages neatly and put them inside the linen envelope. Then I went to shower and get ready. It felt right that finally, at the end of our adventure, we would see the lovers, side by side. Heloise and Abelard.

22

My cherished star. My true one. —*A.*

Harry, August, and I took a cab to the cemetery. "Etienne had to do something at his shop, but he wants to meet us there," Harry said.

I clutched the letter in my hand. I saw August and Harry had theirs.

We arrived at the cemetery. I stared in amazement. The place was crowded. Who knew so many people liked to visit graves? We got a brochure and a map to show precisely where the tomb is. We strolled in the summer heat.

"So what's in your letter, Harry?" I teased.

"A pledge to Gabe. I miss him. Can you believe it? All these years later and I still miss him." Harry shook his head. "True love. Figured I'd leave it here for him. Maybe Heloise and Abelard will watch over us the way they watched over the two of you."

We found the tomb of Heloise and Abelard. It was beautiful, the pergola rising above it, the open arches, the two tombs with their faces carved on them.

I walked over to the wrought-iron railing surrounding it to leave my letter. There were dozens of other letters. I went to put it down and asked August, "Do you want to read it first?"

He shook his head. "I know what's in your heart. But you read mine." He handed me an envelope. "I don't want to be here when you open it. I have something to do. I'll be right back."

I put down my letter, and Harry moved over to Abelard's side of the tomb to place his and to give me some privacy. I picked up August's letter.

Shaking like a branch in a summer storm, I slid my fingernail along the edge to open the envelope.

My darling, my love, my angel,

Calliope was the muse of epic poetry. You are my muse. You are the reason I wake up with a smile on my face, and the reason I go to sleep with a sense of belonging in this world.

All my life, I have felt I didn't belong. I was the boy whose mother didn't want him, whose father was sick. I never felt sorry for myself, but some days, I was just a ghost walking through my own life.

Until the day you showed up.

I can't explain it. You're beautiful, but beyond that your soul is so kind, so understanding, like the things you have been through mean you understand my strange world. For the first time, I actually believe I have someone who fits in my world, and I fit in hers.

I pledge my love to you. Forever, you know. It's not crazy. I know it isn't. We may be young, but we weren't thrown together by just any circumstances. We were united by the quest for the origins of the greatest love story ever. We were united by spirits from a thousand years ago.

And now we'll spend the rest of our lives writing our own love story.

I am forever yours, Calliope, my muse.

Your A.
August

I held the letter and saw a tear drop onto the paper. I didn't even realize I was crying happy tears.

I looked around to show Harry, and to look for August so I could tell him how I felt. Then I saw him.

August. He was walking over a crest in the hill. And he was with Miriam ... and Gabe.

23

One word. Forever.   —A.

Harry flushed three shades of red. "How did you two manage to pull this off?"

I raised my hands. "Don't look at me."

August smiled. "I was in on it."

Gabe smiled. "Miriam and I flew over together. Etienne helped."

The five of us strode over the tomb. It was as if Heloise and Abelard had made sure it all worked out in the end. But one piece was missing.

And then we saw him.

Miriam grabbed onto the wrought-iron railing. I heard her breath catch as Etienne approached, and he suddenly ran toward her. She hugged him and whispered, "It's been too long, my dear."

He tilted her chin up and kissed her on the lips. "We will never be parted again. I should have chased you to New York. I have loved you all this time."

She leaned against him for support. "To think, I never thought I would hear those words."

I took August's hand and walked over so I could see Heloise's face carved on the tomb.

"Thank you," I whispered.

Then, my love by my side, we sealed our pledge with a kiss.

24

My past was over the moment I saw my beloved. I have only her. —A.

Christmas . . . school break, and August and I were closer than ever. We burned bright and hot, but did not burn out. We made long distance work with visits, and I took early decision to NYU.

History major.

My father kept his promise to me. He tries harder now. Though I can't say my majoring in history thrills him, he tells anyone who will listen about his daughter's adventure and find.

The full story of the Book of Hours was the buzz and news of the rare-book and museum community. The entire story was told in a magazine, and the full translation of Astrolabe's writing appeared. A documentary filmmaker even decided to tell the story, complete with interviewing handsome Uncle Harry on camera. The Book of Hours was returned to the monks, as rightfully so, a spoil of the Nazis now safe again.

Astrolabe's story was finally told. It was sadder and more tragic in some ways, than I could have imagined. He did love someone. A beautiful woman named Elizabeth. He was frightened at first. He, like all the world, knew his parents' story. He didn't want to end up like his father, a hermit and bitter until Heloise rescued him from himself. Eventually, though, the pull of his beloved was too much. Despite his fears, he pledged his unending love to her.

Only Astrolabe didn't get the happy ending he deserved. Instead, Elizabeth died when a fever swept through her entire family.

Astrolabe was bereft. But he turned to the only solace he knew. The same solace of his mother. The same solace as his father. He gave his life over to God, eventually becoming a venerable religious man in his own right before his death.

I often wondered, What if Heloise hadn't come to me in my dream? What if the pages had stayed lost forever? Then the world would never know what had become of the child of their love story.

August and I huddled in the blanket in my favorite place. His garden. And we read Astrolabe's words, the lost writings, as reproduced in the magazine.

I am a child born of indiscretion. Born of pain. Born of sorrow. Born of the thorns of the rose, not the bloom.

A child born, though, of a love that defied authority. Defied even God. Defied society. Defied the world.

What is to become of such a child? For two years of my existence, I was given the glorious gift of love. Not just love, but an everlasting passionate love. A rose and jewel. A bright bird and the wind.

My Elizabeth was brighter to me than the sun. She was my stars, my moon, my sun, my crown of light. When she was lost to me, my pain could not be measured in human terms.

To endure, I have given my life over to my heavenly father, to the life of my parents. Of one truth I am convinced.

God gives. He takes away. He reaps. He sows.

I was given Elizabeth so that I would know such a love as my parents'. The whole world does not know such a love. They slumber. A sleepwalking. I want to wake them. Alive! Awake!

Perhaps, though, only one of such a love affair can then bear the loss of such a love. With the great gift from my God was born the great loss. Such as Mary mourned her child, her Son.

I am aware of this.

The heavens may present a crown of stars, and may take that same crown, but the star-crossed lovers have the grandest passion of all.

acknowledgments

As always, to my agent, Jay Poynor, for believing in the story. To my friend Jon Van Zile, for reading the proposal and for the insights offered. To my editor, Jennifer Bonnell—I am truly appreciative of all the direction given to me as I molded a story across a thousand years.

To Alexa . . . who helped me understand my characters and shape their story, and who reminded me of what it means to fall in love.

To my family and the usual suspects—you know who you are.

And especially, to Alexa, Nicholas, Isabella, and Jack . . . in the hopes that you always, for all your lives, believe in love.